To Stella

ORCHARD BOOKS
338 Euston Road, London NW1 3BH
Orchard Books Australia
Level 17/207 Kent Street, Sydney, NSW 2000

ISBN 978 1 40831 952 9

First published in Great Britain in 2012
Text © Keris Stainton 2012

10 9 8 7 6 5 4 3 2 1 (paperback)

Printed in Great Britain

Orchard Books is a division of Hachette Children's Books,
an Hachette UK company.

www.hachette.co.uk

Keris Stainton

ORCHARD

Chapter One

'Most girls of your age would jump at the chance to move to California,' my mum says. She had been standing in front of the fireplace to make the big announcement, but, thanks to my reaction to it, she's now sitting on the sagging sofa next to me.

I stare at her. 'You are joking, right?'

'No. No, I'm not joking,' she says. 'I'm sorry, Emma, but this is a great opportunity for me. And it's a great opportunity for us as a family.'

I glance at my sister, who's sunk deep in a beanbag in the corner of the room. She's fiddling with her phone, a half-smile on her face.

'Bex!' I say. 'You can't be pleased about this! Tell me you're not pleased about this!'

She glances up at me from under her floppy fringe. 'I think it'll be cool to live in Hollywood.'

'Well, it won't actually be Hollywood,' Mum says.

'Near enough,' Bex says, grinning. She's a drama dork, my sister. I bet she thinks she'll be talent-spotted at the airport and have her own Disney XD show by the end of the year.

'It's a new start,' Mum says.

'It's a new start for *you*,' I tell Mum. 'What about me? I don't need a new start. I'm happy here.'

Mum rubs her eyes and then says, 'Oh, damn!' when she realises she's wearing make-up for once and she's just smeared mascara over her face.

'I know,' she says, licking her finger and wiping under her eye. 'I know it's going to be hard for you to leave Bramhall and all your friends, but if you don't come with me, you'll have to live with your dad, so—'

'I'm not doing that,' I interrupt. And then I roll my eyes. 'I'm not saying I'm not coming. I know I have to come. I'm just not happy about it.'

'And you've made that perfectly clear,' Mum says.

'What does Dad think about it anyway?' I ask. 'Did he suggest we go live with him instead?'

'Not exactly, no,' Mum says, which I know means 'not at all'.

Bex's head snaps up from her phone – she's obviously been texting all her friends: OMG! MOVIN 2 LA!

'What did he say?' she asks Mum.

'He's all for it,' Mum says, and rubs her eyes again. 'I mean, obviously he's not thrilled that you're going to be so far away, but he sees what a great opportunity it is and he thinks a new start will be good for all of us.'

'He'll be able to come and visit, won't he?' Bex says. Her cheeks have gone red, probably because she was so busy texting in her excitement, she forgot all about Dad.

'Of course,' Mum says. 'And we'll come home when we can too.'

'And he'll be able to get on with his new life without having to worry about us,' I say. 'Does he still have to pay maintenance if we move thousands of miles away?'

'That's between me and your father,' Mum

says, rubbing the back of her neck and rolling her shoulders back.

She looks so tired that I feel bad for acting like such a brat.

'Is it a really good job?' I ask her.

Her face lights up and she looks years younger. 'It's an incredibly opportunity. I wouldn't even consider doing this if it wasn't – you know that. I'm going to be working on the properties and evolution of young high-mass stars and—'

'Where will we live?' I interrupt. I know from past experience if Mum starts talking about her research we'll be here all day. 'Somewhere better than this?'

Mum pulls a face. 'I would hope so. Don't worry, we'll find somewhere really nice, I promise.'

I close my eyes and try to picture myself in LA. Lying on the beach. Rollerblading in Malibu. Shopping on Rodeo Drive. For some reason my subconscious has given me enormous fake boobs.

I open my eyes and look around this room, with its peeling wallpaper, threadbare carpet and view of the redbrick wall of the factory opposite.

'If we really, really hate it...' I start.

'We can come home, of course,' Mum says.

'OK,' I say. 'I'll give it a try.'

Mum drops her arm around my shoulders and gives me a quick squeeze. 'Thank you.'

The house phone rings and she rushes to the kitchen to answer it. I scuff a torn bit of carpet with my shoe and think about telling my friends that I'm moving to LA. I'm not sure they'll really care. My friends are great, but my best friend Jessie moved to New York last year and I certainly haven't replaced her. It'll be funny, us both being over there. But I think LA is actually further from New York than we are now. Still, we'll be in the same continent, at least.

'Do you really think Dad wants to get rid of us?' Bex asks.

She's still got the two little red smudges on her cheeks that she always gets when she's angry or upset.

'Not really,' I say. 'Or not permanently, anyway.'

'Why don't you want to go, Em?' she says, as her phone beeps and she glances at the screen. 'It sounds so cool.'

'I'm sure it'll be great,' I say, getting my own phone out of my pocket. 'I've just had enough of change this year.'

'I know what you mean, but that's all been bad change. This will be good change.' She grins at me and goes back to texting.

I head up to my room, tripping over the loose bit of stair carpet as I do almost every single time I pass it. I hear Mum on the phone saying, 'That sounds incredible. And how much is it?' and wonder who she's talking to.

In our old house, my room was my sanctuary. If ever I was upset or worried or angry, I felt better in my room. Mum and Dad let me choose pretty much everything for it and it was so me. It had a bay window with a window seat, built-in bookshelves and a fireplace that I'd filled with candles. I put framed pictures on the walls rather than posters and I had this huge starburst mirror that Dad found at a car-boot sale and knew I'd love. Back when he cared about what made me happy.

My room here is bigger than my old room, but that's about the only thing in its favour. It's just plain and square and boring. And painted magnolia. The mirror and the pictures are packed up now, we're not allowed to hang anything on the walls in this house because it's rented and, according to the landlord, the brick is too soft. But there's no point in thinking about it. Things change. I have to get used to that idea. Jessie's parents split up a couple of years ago and her mum and dad both found themselves boyfriends, so I should know better than to expect everything to stay the same.

I lie down on the bed and text Jessie. It actually worked out really well for her, eventually. Her mum had moved to New York and now they're all living there – her mum and her boyfriend, her dad and his boyfriend, and Jessie and her boyfriend, Finn. Not all together, obviously. But they're all really happy. Much happier than when her parents were still married, Jessie says.

I tell Jessie to Skype me when she gets a chance and then I stare up at the enormous water stain on my bedroom ceiling. It looks a bit like America, if I squint.

Chapter Two

'Oh my god, that's so exciting!' Jessie says.

I'm sitting up in bed with my knackered netbook on my knee. It usually crashes every few minutes, but for some reason it works fine with Skype.

I snort. 'You sound like Bex.'

'Oh, I bet Bex is beside herself, isn't she?'

'Yep. She's probably googling "child-star agency representation" and watching *High School Musical* as we speak.'

Jessie laughs. 'And how do you feel about it? Not keen?'

'Not really, no. It's just too much change, you know?'

'I do, yeah. But, you know, you hate where you live and it could be a really good change. And if it doesn't work out you can always come home...'

'Now you sound like Mum.'

'I know,' Jessie says. 'I'm sorry. But what else can you do? You may as well try to enjoy it. It's LA, after all!'

'Yeah, I've been watching Ryan Gosling paparazzi videos on YouTube to try to convince myself.'

'And if that doesn't convince you, I don't know what will,' Jessie says, before adding, '"Hey, Girl..."'

I laugh. It's from this Ryan Gosling Tumblr she sent me that we're both obsessed with.

'"Hey, Girl,"' I say, in my best fake Ryan Gosling voice, '"I know you're scared about moving to LA. Would it help if I met you at the airport?"'

Jessie snorts and then sighs. Neither of us has any idea of what Ryan Gosling's really like, obviously, but we're both in love with the internet's version.

'I remember you telling me on the way to New York that it was the place to find a boy,' she says. 'And you were right, weren't you? I bet LA is teeming with hot boys—'

'Yeah, and surgically enhanced women. I'm not sure grumpy and pasty is going to go down all that well.'

She laughs. 'Oh, you never know. Grumpy and pasty might be the new hipster thing... And you don't look pasty anyway. You look great, as usual.'

I pull a face. 'I don't. I'm pale and spotty.' I point to a spot under my chin. Jessie looks fantastic – her long, wavy hair is glossy and she's so much more groomed than when she lived in Manchester.

'Well, there you go!' Jessie says. 'You need some sun.'

'And I'm certainly going to get some.'

We're both quiet for a few seconds, then Jessie frowns and I know exactly what she's going to say.

'Have you talked to your dad about it?' she asks.

Yep. Knew it.

'Not yet,' I tell her.

'But you *are* going to?'

'I don't know. He'll want to see us before we go, obviously.'

'Em, you really need to talk to him,' Jessie says.

I shake my head. 'I don't know what to say to him.'

'Just tell him how you feel. You said that to me when me and Mum weren't really speaking and you were absolutely right. I can't believe you're doing the same thing now.'

'I know,' I say. 'I will speak to him, honest.'

'Things won't get any better if you keep avoiding him,' she says.

'They're not going to get better anyway, are they? They'll still have split up. He'll still be with someone else. We'll still be thousands of miles away.'

'I know. But you'll feel better about it. I promise.'

After we've talked for a while I go downstairs to find Mum. She's sitting at the kitchen table and writing a list on one of the big yellow notepads she loves. She looks up at me and for a second I'm startled – she looks like she's been crying. It could just be that she's rubbed all her mascara off, but I give her a hug just in case.

'I'm sorry I was such a cow,' I say. 'Shall I make you a cup of coffee?'

She sighs, making the pages of her pad flutter. 'Yes. Please. Although I don't think I'll get much sleep tonight anyway. Coffee's the last thing I need.'

'I could do you a hot chocolate...' I say, opening the kitchen cupboard, forgetting that the door's loose. It crashes down onto the countertop and Mum jumps.

'We should just take that one off the hinge,' she says.

'Sorry, I should've remembered it's knackered.'

I get the jar of hot chocolate out and spoon it into Mum's favourite mug (it has THE PHYSICS IS THEORETICAL, BUT THE FUN IS REAL on it and it's so geeky it always makes me smile) before filling the kettle.

'That was Michael on the phone earlier,' Mum says. 'He's found us a house.'

Michael got Mum the job and he also happens to be Dad's best friend. He and my parents worked together at the Jodrell Bank Observatory and then he got a job at UCLA and moved out there with his wife, Jackie, and their son, Oscar. And then Michael and Jackie split up too and Jackie moved to somewhere near San Francisco. Oscar stayed with his dad in LA because he was happy at school there. Michael and Jackie are still really good friends, apparently – they've even been away on holiday together. Mum and Dad used to joke about it, before they split up too.

Mum pulls her hair out of its low ponytail. 'It's near his house and he says it's a wonderful area. Says you two girls will love it.'

'So you're going to be working with Michael? And we're going to be living next door to him?' I stir the hot chocolate. 'Is there something you want to tell me?'

Mum snorts. 'God, no, nothing like that. I've known Michael since university! And it's not next door, it's just nearby. He's been a really good friend to me since your father...left. And you're friends with Oscar, so...'

I roll my eyes. 'I haven't even spoken to him for about five years!'

'I know, but you always got on so well. It'll be nice for you to have a friend out there.'

I put the hot chocolate down in front of Mum and start making one for myself.

Oscar and I were quite good friends for a few years, but it was one of those friendships you just grow out of. I started spending more time with

Jessie, and Oscar was always such a dork. He never wanted to do the same things we did – he was always doing projects based on his dad's research – so we just kind of stopped hanging out. I sent him a card when his parents split up and I always meant to email him, but I never got around to it. And then it just seemed like I'd left it too long. I wonder what he's like now. I bet he's exactly the same.

Chapter Three

I put it off all weekend, but I promised Mum I'd do it before the end of the week, so on Sunday evening, I ring my dad's mobile. It rings six times – I count – before being answered with a scuffling noise, as if he picked it up and immediately dropped it.

'Emma?'

It's not Dad. It's Clare. Exactly who I'd been trying to avoid by ringing his mobile.

I've only just managed to say 'Yeah...' when Clare says, 'He's just upstairs. Hold on. I'll get him. I know he's really keen to...he's really looking forward to talking to you.'

'OK.'

She doesn't chat as she goes off to find him, which I appreciate. She seems like a nice enough person, but we've only met a couple of times at the customary 'getting to know the children/ new girlfriend' lunches, so small talk seems a bit pointless.

I hear her go up the stairs and I try to picture where his study is in their house – Clare's house – but I can't quite remember. I've only been there once. I know it's a box room that Clare used for an exercise bike and a rowing machine before Dad moved in, but she put them in the garage and now she parks her car on the street.

I hear the music, so I know she's getting closer – it's 'Venus' from Holst's *The Planets*. Mum always laughed at him for listening to it so much – she said it was the cheesiest thing for an astrophysicist to love – but he always has it on when he works. He says it helps him focus. It's how I always knew whether or not he was at home when I came in from school – no Holst meant no Dad. I haven't heard it since he left.

If Clare says anything I miss it because the music

stops and the next thing I hear is Dad's voice, saying 'Emma?'

I feel a painful clenching in my stomach and then the pain's replaced by butterflies. I never thought I'd get butterflies talking to my dad. Never.

'Hi,' I say, and it comes out in a whisper.

'How are you?'

'I'm...fine. Thanks. How are you?'

'Good, thanks. Sorry, I left my phone downstairs. I'm working on a protostar study and practically everything else has gone out of my head.'

I nod. He was always like that. They both were – he and Mum. Me and Bex used to call them 'spaceheads'.

'So,' he says. 'LA.'

'Yep.'

'Sounds very exciting. It's an incredible opportunity for your mum.'

'So she keeps telling me,' I say. 'And for Bex too, I think. She's already talking about meetings with agents.'

'Yes,' he says. 'Bex told me.'

I always forget that Bex talks to him much more than I do. Bex is more resilient, that's what I heard

Mum say on the phone one day. Bex takes things in her stride. The suggestion being, I suppose, that I don't. But there are some things that are too big to just accept, aren't there?

'How do you feel about it?' Dad asks.

'I'm getting used to the idea,' I tell him. 'Mum and Bex both seem really happy and, you know, we can always come back if it doesn't work out.'

'Of course,' he says. 'You know you don't have to go if you don't want to? You know you could come here?'

My eyes fill with tears and I have to swallow a couple of times before I can speak.

'Emma?' he says. I picture him with his elbows on his desk, frowning into the phone, and I can't believe he's living somewhere else with someone else. It just seems impossible.

'No,' I say. 'I want to go.'

Chapter Four

It takes ages to get through LAX and we're all
yawning as we queue at immigration. I'd thought I'd
be able to sleep on the plane, but I was freezing – they
turned the heating off when we went through some
turbulence because it stops people being sick, but
after they turned it on it took ages to warm up again
– and I just couldn't manage to get comfortable.
Mum and Bex both slept on and off while I watched
random episodes of *The Big Bang Theory* and *How
I Met Your Mother* and thought about how long it was
taking. LA really is the other side of the world.

I can't quite believe we're going to be living so far
away from Dad. Not that I particularly want to see

him at the moment, but it just seems wrong. What if something happens to him? What if something happens to one of us? It's almost a day away. I keep thinking of when I was little and I fell over in the playground at school and hit my face on the kerb between the concrete and the grass. It knocked one of my teeth out – it was a baby tooth and it had been loose anyway – and burst my bottom lip. I remember sitting on the ground and wailing. I was really shocked that the blood was so warm, running down my chin. I remember seeing one of the teachers running across the playground towards me, which made me cry even harder because she looked so scared, and then the next thing I remember is sitting on my dad's knee in the Head's office. He was holding a paper towel with ice in it to my face and whispering in my ear that I was fine, everything was OK.

It must have taken him at least ten minutes to get there, even if he'd been working at home, but it had seemed to me that I was hurt and then Dad was there. Almost instantly. And I felt better. And now he's tens of thousands of miles away. If I could've told my six-year-old self, sitting on the playground, that one day Dad would fall in love with someone else and leave us, she wouldn't have believed it. I still don't believe it, and I'm ten years older.

'You're quiet,' Mum says to me, as we finally make it through immigration – which is intimidating: the officers wear dark glasses, and we have to be fingerprinted and have our retinas scanned.

'I'm tired,' I tell her. Which is true, but not really why I've been quiet.

She stops walking and looks at me and Bex.

'Are we ready for this?' she says. Her eyes are sparkling, so I know she is.

'Absolutely,' Bex says, grinning.

'Ready as I'll ever be,' I say.

Michael is waiting for us in Arrivals, holding a piece of card with WELCOME TO LA written on it.

Michael hugs Mum and then just looks at me and Bex. 'Wow,' he says. 'You girls are growing up.'

'Yep,' I say. 'It happens.'

'Is Oscar with you?' Mum asks, ignoring me.

He shakes his head. 'He wanted to come, but he had to work. He's really looking forward to seeing you all, though. Shall we go?'

Michael grabs the luggage trolley and wheels it towards the automatic doors. And I don't move. I feel like I've been punched. We look like a family. If anyone was watching they'd think we were his wife and daughters joining him in LA. They'd think Mum and Michael were married. They'd think Michael was our dad.

I see Bex turn as if she's going to say something and then she realises I'm not there and turns around. She frowns and heads back towards me.

'What's wrong?'

'Look at them,' I say. I point, limply.

'What?'

'We look like a family.'

Bex puts her arm through mine and squeezes. 'Em, Michael is Dad's best friend. He's Mum's friend. He's not trying to replace Dad.'

I know she's right. It's not that I think there's anything going on between Mum and Michael, because I don't, but it still seems wrong. We used to be two families: Michael, Jackie and Oscar, and Mum, Dad, Bex and me, and now we're all blown apart. Why does everyone have to move on all the time? Couldn't we at least just stay still until we'd got used to everything? It's like I'm on one of those moving walkways in the airport. I've stopped, but everything else is still moving and I'm going to get thrown off at the end, flat on my face.

We go through the double doors and the heat hits me like a wet towel in the face – a hot wet towel, like the ones we got on the plane after dinner...or was it breakfast? I start sweating immediately and I can feel my face getting redder and redder. I'm so not cut out for this place.

'Isn't it glorious?' Mum says, turning her face up to the sun.

We wait outside in the shade while Michael goes to get the car.

It's really busy. Cars swerve and honk and a series of car-hire transfer buses pull up nearby. On the other side of the road there are palm trees, which seems strange among all this concrete.

Michael pulls up next to us in an ordinary-looking

silver car and piles our cases in the boot. All our other things are being shipped and probably won't be here for about six weeks.

'Ooh, you've got a Prius?' Mum says, and Michael spends the next five minutes telling her all about how much more efficient and economical this car is than his old one, while Bex and I fiddle with our phones. I've got a text and I click on it, hoping it's from Jessie, but it's actually from the local mobile provider welcoming me to LA.

Once we've managed to get out of the snarl of airport traffic and onto the main road, Bex tells Michael about the meeting she's got set up with a casting agent. Vivienne, the woman who owns Starmakers, the stage school Bex has been going to for years, arranged it. I always assumed Vivienne's stories about her own acting career were exaggerated to inspire her pupils, but Mum and Bex have spoken to the agent – who's actually flown over in the past to see some of Starmakers' stage shows – and she's said she's interested in sending Bex out on some castings.

As Bex talks, I stare out of the window with

a weird sense of déjà vu. Pretty much this time last year I was with Jessie going to New York for the summer. We were both so excited about spending the summer as good as parent-free (Jessie's mum was much too busy to worry about what we were up to) and about possibly meeting amazing boys. Jessie met Finn and now they're totally loved-up, but I didn't meet anyone at all, unless you count the guy in the deli who looked like an older, fatter Joey Tribbiani and was possibly more into Jessie than me anyway. I never seem to meet anyone. Or at least no one I like who also likes me.

We turn down a series of nondescript streets. I can tell we're in America because of the shops – Radio Shack, Walgreens, Sprint – but there's nothing to suggest we're in LA – no paparazzi or Hollywood sign, just boring shiny high-rise buildings and yet more palm trees. And then we turn off into a residential street lined on both sides with bungalows. It reminds me a bit of the estate we used to live on, before Mum and Dad split up. Michael, Jackie and Oscar lived there too, before they moved to LA. The roads are much wider here than at home, but the houses are quite similar. It gives me a funny feeling in my stomach, like we've taken our old life and moved it to LA. And then the road narrows and the houses are closer together and it starts to look like the Caribbean – little balconies and smaller palm trees and—

'Oh, *wow!*' Bex cries.

I see it just a second after she does – a white wooden bridge over a river. Each side of the river is lined with houses, every one different: a modern, square building painted bright blue stands next to a huge white villa with balconies and columns. Some of the houses have little wooden jetties poking out onto the water and a few even have kayaks tied up. I had no idea there was anything like this in LA.

'Where are we?' I find myself asking.

'Well, we're not quite there yet,' Michael says from the driving seat, 'but it's almost your new home.'

We cross another bridge and then another and then pass a small children's playground which is where a sign tells me these aren't rivers at all, but canals. I knew we were coming to live in Venice, but it never occurred to me that there'd be canals, like the *real* Venice. We turn off into a side street and pass yet more odd and mismatched houses. Some are painted bright colours, others look unfinished, and a few are plain concrete and look more like multi-storey car parks than anyone's home. And then Michael pulls over to a grey painted house on the left and says, 'Here we are.'

I feel a clutch of disappointment that we're not actually staying on a canal, but I don't say anything. Those houses probably cost a fortune. At least we're near enough that we can walk around the canals. I can't wait to check them out.

I get out of the car and turn in a circle to take in our new neighbourhood. Directly opposite our house is a building site: enormous rickety-looking metal gates with KEEP OUT signs. In the gaps I can see a half-built building and a portaloo. Lovely.

'This is so exciting!' Bex says, grabbing my arm.

I give her a look and she rolls her eyes at me.

'How far away is your house?' she asks Michael as we follow him under the carport to the back door.

'Back there, off the road before we turned on to the canals. Not far at all.' He steps back and gestures for Mum, Bex and me to go through the door in front of him.

'The utility room is through there,' he says, gesturing right, as we all follow him down a dingy hallway, but then he opens a door to the kitchen and Mum says, 'Oh my god!'

The kitchen's light and bright and about four times the size of the kitchen in our rented house and twice the size of Mum's perfect kitchen in our old home. And when I see the living room I hear myself gasp. It's got a wood-burning stove, wooden floors, a beamed ceiling and enormous windows through which I can see – I cross the room in about five giant steps – the canal.

'It's on the canal!' Bex shrieks.

It really is. There's a door out onto a terrace overlooking the canal. We all troop out there and stand staring.

'So what do you think?' Michael says, but he looks really smug; he knows full well we're going to love this house.

'It's fantastic,' I say, and he reaches over and squeezes my shoulder.

It makes me miss my dad. I wonder what he'd think of this place. I can't really picture him sitting out on this deck, having coffee and reading the paper. I can picture myself out here, though.

'Shall we have a look at the rest of the house?' Michael says.

We follow him back through to the hallway and up some narrow stairs. The bedrooms are just as gorgeous as the rooms downstairs and they all lead out onto another terrace with sunbeds.

'It's absolutely perfect,' Mum tells Michael as Bex goes from corner to corner looking at the view and I hang back – I don't like heights.

'There might be some noise from the building works over there,' Michael says, gesturing over the back of the house towards the site I saw when we first pulled up, 'which is why it came in a lot cheaper than the other houses. But it shouldn't be too bad, at least in the evenings and weekends anyway.'

'It's wonderful,' Mum says. 'Thank you so much for sorting this out.'

'It was my pleasure,' he says.

Once Michael's left to let us get unpacked and

settle in, Mum puts her arms around me and my sister. 'So what do you think? Better than you expected?'

'Much better,' I say. 'I was expecting one of those apartment blocks around a pool with a dead body floating in it.'

Mum laughs and squeezes me. 'My little optimist.'

Chapter Five

I wake up to the sound of birdsong and a weird whirring noise I can't quite place. Then I open my eyes and remember – the ceiling fan. I stretch my feet down to the bottom of the bed and look over to my right where I left a space in the curtains so I could look out and remind myself of exactly where we've ended up living.

You wouldn't know we were in the middle of not only a city, but an enormous city – all I can see is the wooden terrace, trees and sky. It's gorgeous. I jump as something taps against the window and drag myself out of bed to check. If it's a raccoon I'm getting on the next flight home. I pull my curtain back slowly, squinting as if that'll protect me from whatever's out there, but it turns out it's just Bex. She's wearing a Justin Bieber T-shirt (she says it's ironic – I'm not so sure) and her school gym shorts.

'What the hell are you doing?' I ask her through the glass.

She gestures at me to open the door, so I do before crossing the room and getting back in my bed.

'Yoga!' she says, bounding into my room like Tigger. 'I thought we could do it every morning. You know, on the terrace?'

'Feel free,' I say.

'No! Both of us! I think it'll be really good! We can have some sister bonding time. You can get a bit more flexible, you know?'

'I don't need to be more flexible,' I say, burrowing down under the covers. 'I'm as flexible as I want to be.'

'It's good for you!' Bex says. 'This is California. Beautiful people! You need to step it up!'

'Why do I?' I say. I can hear a weird thudding noise. I open one eye. She's actually running on the spot.

'Because we're in LA now!' she says, and starts stretching. 'I'm going to get fit. I'm going to start running, and Mum says she'll get me a bike. Or maybe some rollerblades. Do you think people really do rollerblade at the beach? Like in films?'

'I wouldn't be at all surprised,' I tell her. 'But you're on your own.'

'Fine,' she says, and I hear her cross the room again. 'But just for today. You're joining me tomorrow.'

'Whatever.'

I go back to sleep.

When I finally get up, Mum and Bex are sitting on the deck downstairs. Mum's writing a list.

'Sleep well?' Mum asks.

'Really well,' I tell her. I was surprised because I went to bed thinking about home and Dad and how different everything is here, so I expected to lie awake for ages, but I think I must've fallen asleep straight away. The bed is really comfy. 'You?'

'Great,' she says. 'I think we were all worn out from the journey.'

'You didn't expect to sleep either?' I ask her.

She shakes her head. 'I thought I'd be too worried. You know, about work and this house and driving in LA!' She makes a horrified face. 'I suppose I can just worry about that today instead.'

'Has the university got a car for you?' I ask her.

She nods. 'Michael sorted that out too. Didn't you see it when we got here? It's a blue Mini.'

'I didn't notice.' I was probably too busy looking at the building site and the bins.

'Do you need anything?' she asks, pointing at her list with the pen. 'We're going to walk up to the shop. Michael left us a map.'

'No thanks, I'm going to have a shower and unpack.'

Mum and Bex head off with their list and I sit and look out at the canal. Directly opposite our house, four little boats are tied up and pointing out into the water. One's a kayak, and the others are rowing boats. There's a bird sitting on each one – two huge white birds that might be herons and two smaller brown ones with curved yellow beaks. I can hear the water lapping against the plastic. The birds shift from foot to foot and ruffle their feathers.

I hear voices and splashing and I go to the gate

to look down the canal. Obviously people must use these boats otherwise they wouldn't be here, but I can't imagine who. The boat that's coming towards me looks like one of the rafts we made on an outward-bound course the school forced us on a couple of years ago. It's like two kayaks held together by planks of wood. Two men in high-vis jackets are standing on each kayak and holding fishing nets. At first I think they are actually fishing, but as they come closer I realise they're cleaning the canal. And there's a little motor at the back of the boat.

Then behind them, on the opposite side of the canal, I see Oscar. I know it's him immediately, even though he's got bright red hair – like tomato red – and his hair used to be mousy brown. It's something about the way he walks – it's kind of loose and relaxed, but nervous at the same time, as if someone's following him but he doesn't want them to know he knows. I think about shouting his name, but it's so peaceful here that it seems wrong. As I watch him, he bends over and starts walking really slowly, as if he's tracking something.

I get up, step into my flip-flops, grab the keys Mum left for me, and pull the door closed. By the time I reach the canal path, Oscar's gone out of sight, so I hurry along, hoping I'll still be able to see him round the corner. When I get to the bridge, I spot him. He's walking slowly, sort of bent double, and he seems to be talking to himself.

As I cross the bridge, a huge bird lands right in front of me. It's pure white with bright yellow rubbery-looking feet and a really pointy beak. I stop and stare at it. It stares back at me. But when I take a step to carry on towards Oscar, it flies right for me. I gasp with shock, the bird skirts right over the top of my head and then I'm choking. I think I've swallowed – or not quite swallowed, obviously – a fly. I'm gasping for air, coughing and clutching at my throat.

'Emma?' I hear. I've got my eyes closed. 'What are you doing?'

I open my eyes and cough violently again. Oscar's standing at the bottom of the bridge looking up at me. 'I swallowed a fly,' I croak.

'Ah,' he says. 'You know what you need to do?'

'If you say "swallow a spider" I'll have to kill you.'

'Oh.' He looks thoughtful. 'I can't help you then.' He grins and for a second I'm a bit startled – he's so much better-looking than he used to be. His features always seemed too big for his face, but he's obviously grown into them because now he's definitely cute. I wasn't expecting that.

'What are you doing?' I ask, gesturing at the bit of the canal where he was doing his weird walking.

'Oh,' he says. 'You saw that. I was just seeing the ducks home.' At least he has the decency to look a bit embarrassed.

'Pardon?'

'The ducks!' He gestures around the corner.

'You've lost me,' I say.

He sets off walking and I follow him. Just round the corner are two ducks standing on the pavement. They're looking back at Oscar as if awaiting further instructions.

'They wander away from the pond and then can't get home,' he says. 'They do seem to be particularly stupid ducks.'

As if to underline this, another big bird flies past,

causing the ducks to flutter about six inches off the ground in panic.

'It's OK,' Oscar says soothingly to the ducks. 'They're nervous wrecks,' he says to me.

Without actually thinking about it, I find myself bent over like Oscar, creeping along after two neurotic ducks.

'How far is it?' I whisper.

'Not far,' Oscar whispers back. 'Why are we whispering?'

'I don't know. It just seemed like a whispering occasion.'

About two minutes later we turn another corner and are faced with the children's playground we passed yesterday and, next to it, a small pond full of much less gormless ducks.

'There you go!' Oscar says. The ducks flutter gratefully into the water. 'You should maybe just think about staying here, yeah?'

The ducks stare at him as if they're genuinely listening. They really do.

I laugh. 'What are you? Some kind of duck whisperer?'

'Ah,' Oscar says, 'we can all talk to the animals as long as we believe.'

'Yeah,' I say, grinning. 'Course we can.'

'You seem to have forgotten that I taught my budgie to talk and you, madam, did not.'

'You taught your budgie one measly word,' I tell him. 'Not impressed.'

'It was still one more word than you managed to teach yours,' he says, bumping his arm against mine.

'It wasn't even a good word,' I say. 'You could've at least taught it to say "bollocks" or something.'

'"Hello" was a perfectly reasonable first word to teach it.'

'Yeah, first word. Not only word.'

'Well, I really didn't expect it to be his only word. I thought I'd have him chatting away in no time.'

I laugh and remember the look on Oscar's face when he'd first spotted my budgie, Nipper. Nipper was grey and white and really sweet. Oscar was obsessed and nagged his parents until they gave in and bought him his own budgie. His was green and yellow and he named him Busby. Nipper showed no inclination to talk at all. All he wanted to do was chew up newspaper and look at himself in the mirror. But Busby used to sit on Oscar's finger for hours, watching his mouth as he chattered away.

I used to take the piss out of him and call him the Mad Bird Boy of Bramhall. Which was a bit rich now I think about it, since I bloody loved Nipper. When he died, I was so upset I got sent home from school. And I was in Year 8.

As we turn to walk back to the canal, I shade my eyes and say, 'What are you wearing?'

He looks down at himself and then back up at me. 'What?' But he's grinning, so he knows exactly what I'm getting at.

He's wearing baggy long shorts and a sort of tank top over a T-shirt with bright green trainers and no socks. He always did dress weird – as if he couldn't care less what anyone thought – but not this weird. He's also got a sort of barrel bag over his back with badges pinned to the strap. One of them says WE ARE ALL MADE OF STARDUST.

'More to the point, what are *you* wearing?' he says.

I glance down at myself and feel my cheeks get hot. In my rush to find out what Oscar was doing I didn't even realise what I'd left the house in. I'm wearing a black T-shirt over Elmo pyjama bottoms.

'I may have Elmo on my pyjamas, but you appear to have him on your head,' I say.

He reaches up and runs his hand through his red hair. 'Oh yeah. I did this for a bet, but I like it. What do you think? It's eye-catching, right?'

'Almost eye-searing,' I say.

He grins and points to his teeth. 'No brace either.'

His teeth are straight and his grin is just as huge as it always was. People used to call him Banana Mouth.

I realise I'm grinning back at him without even thinking about it.

He sort of pats me on the arm and hops up and down a little bit. 'It's so good to see you!' he says.

'You too,' I say.

And it is.

Chapter Six

Oscar had been on his way to see us when he'd spotted the lost ducks, so he walks back with me. Mum used to have this little wooden plaque on the wall in the kitchen – someone had given it to her at work as a jokey Secret Santa thing. It said, FRIENDS ARE LIKE STARS. JUST BECAUSE YOU CAN'T SEE THEM, DOESN'T MEAN THEY'RE NOT THERE. It pops into my head now and I actually roll my eyes, it's so lame. But Oscar and I chat so easily that it's as if I only saw him last week, rather than a few years ago.

I go through the gate and Oscar stands on the fence, like a kid. 'What do you think of the house?'

'It's great,' I say. 'I can't believe how quiet it is here.'

Oscar follows me onto the terrace and I open the door. 'Mum and Bex must still be out. They went to get some stuff at the shop.'

I kick off my flip-flops, sit down and put my feet on the chair opposite.

'I was sorry to hear about your mum and dad,' Oscar says.

I glance at him and he's looking at me really intently. I'd forgotten he's quite intense about eye contact.

'Thanks,' I say.

'It must have been a shock.'

I shrug. 'It was, yeah. How are things with your parents?'

'Good, thanks. Mum lives in San Luis Obispo now. I go up there quite a lot. It's a really cool place.'

'She's got a boyfriend?'

He nods. 'Jack. He's great. Bit of a hippie, but he makes Mum really happy.'

'Jack and Jackie?' I say, smiling.

He grins. 'Terrible, isn't it?'

We all knew Oscar's parents weren't happy when we were growing up. They never fought in front of us, but they used to snap at each other a lot and often there was a horrible atmosphere in their house. I can clearly remember being in the car on our way home from visiting Oscar's family and hearing my mum and dad talking about his parents' marriage. It was, I think, the first time I heard of anyone 'staying together for the sake of the children' and I remember my mum saying that it wasn't doing Oscar any good to live in that sort of environment. I remember feeling sorry for Oscar after that and, for a while, wondering if I should suggest Oscar could come to live with us. Because we were a really happy family. Then.

'And what about your dad?' I ask.

'He's fine with it. They're both a lot happier now, so...'

'No, I meant has he got a girlfriend?'

He laughs. 'Oh, right. Sorry! No. No time. He works a lot. I hope your mum's prepared for UCLA. If you thought they were workaholics before...' He pulls a horrified face.

'She'll love it,' I say. 'I bet she would've gone in today if she could've.'

'And what about you? Are you looking forward to...?' He waves his hand to indicate everything.

I look around. It's warm and quiet and, on the surface, completely blissful, but... 'I don't know. I really didn't want to come...'

'I know,' he says. 'My dad told me. I'll try not to take it personally.'

I laugh. 'Yeah, don't. It's just a long way, you know? And I just couldn't picture myself here at all. I could see myself in New York, but not here.'

'I thought that when we moved here too,' Oscar says. 'Also, it just didn't seem like my kind of place, you know? All surfers and egg-white omelettes and plastic surgery?' He shakes his head.

'Exactly,' I say. 'And I was worried about everything being fake and obsessed with celebrities. I couldn't even picture LA as a real place. I mean, where real people live. Does that sound stupid?'

'No, I know exactly what you mean. I couldn't picture it before we moved here either, but it's not so much one big city, it's more like lots of little communities. Venice is different to Brentwood which is different to Silver Lake...'

I nod. 'You remember Jessie? She lives right in the middle of New York. It's just a few blocks from Central Park, not far from Times Square, but she knows her neighbours, she knows the people in the shops...'

'It's up to you how much of it you want to experience,' Oscar says. 'I pretty much stick to Venice and Santa Monica. I live here, I work here, I hang out here and my friends are here. Hollywood and all that hoo-ha doesn't really have an impact on me. Except when there's filming down here and then that's just as entertaining as it would be at home.'

I smile at him. 'I wish I'd spoken to you before we even set off. That makes me feel much better about it all.'

He does a sort of half-bow in his seat and smiles.

I hear a helicopter and I look up, shading my eyes.

'You get used to them,' he says. 'They go over quite a lot.'

'What are they?'

'Could be news crews or the traffic copter. Or

some celebrity who's too important for the speed limit...'

'Was it hard for you, moving?' I ask him. He seems so comfortable here, it's really surprising.

He shrugs. 'It was a bit, yeah. To begin with everyone just seemed so cool – I thought no one would ever speak to me – but you'd be surprised at how far an English accent gets you...' He gives me a little grin. 'So school was easier than I thought it would be...most of the time. How's Bex? She wanted to move, right?'

'I think she thinks she's going to be discovered. She's already got meetings set up, you know? And she wants us to do yoga on the terrace together every morning.'

Oscar laughs. 'Really? Wow. Usually it takes a little longer than a day to get the whole LA health bug...' He fiddles with the badges on his bag.

'You've got it?' I ask him, grinning.

He laughs again. 'I have been known to ride a bike...'

I burst out laughing. Our dads actually taught us to ride bikes together and Oscar was sort of infamous in our family for being absolutely hopeless at it. He had stabilisers until he was about ten when he finally decided it was all too humiliating and gave it up as a bad job. I was secretly pleased because I'd mainly heard from my parents how much better at pretty much everything Oscar was than me. Even stupid things like blowing his nose. I'd blow my nose, blowing more out of my mouth, and my dad would say, 'Oscar can blow his nose properly, Emma, I don't know why you can't.' And I used to wish we never had to see Oscar at all.

He's still grinning at me.

'They don't even point at my stabilisers here,' he says, and I laugh again. He always did have a sense of humour about himself. I'd forgotten that.

I hear 'Hi, Oscar!' from inside the house and then Bex appears. She's wearing a sundress and Converse boots.

'Hey! You look great!' Oscar says, and Bex twirls.

Mum comes through and I swing my legs down from the seat opposite so she can sit down, but Oscar leaps up and hugs her. It's a bit disorientating how much he's changed. He used to be so shy around my parents. He'd be chatting away in my room, but if one of them came in, he'd immediately stop – sometimes part-way through a word – and blush. To be fair, once it was when I'd convinced Oscar to let me paint his nails, but even when we weren't doing anything embarrassing, he'd still clam up. And now here he is chatting to Mum just like a normal person.

'So are you busy now?' Oscar asks. 'I thought I could show you round Venice. Save you looking too much like tourists.'

Mum shakes her head. 'That's really sweet of you. I've got a few things I need to do – more than a few things, actually – but you should take these two.' She gestures at me and Bex. 'I'll feel better leaving them tomorrow if I know they can find their way to the beach at least.'

I roll my eyes – I'm pretty sure we'd be able to find the beach without Oscar's help – but I leave them to catch up and go up to shower and get dressed.

Half an hour later, Bex and I are following Oscar back down onto the canal path. He takes us over a different bridge and then along a path made of round paving stones, like stepping stones. It's between two really weird houses – one seems to be wooden but has actual turrets along the top. The other is pink and orange and blue and looks like boxes, piled haphazardly. Even the wheelie bins are spray-painted with stripes.

'What is it with all these houses?' I say.

'It was the 60s, man,' Oscar says in a stoner voice. 'You weren't there, man! You weren't there!'

I snort and he grins at me.

'This place used to be a proper hippie hangout,' he says, 'but then it got cleaned up and now it's much more exclusive. You have some actual celebrity neighbours, apparently. Not that I've ever seen them.'

We cross the road and head down another narrow path between buildings. We're about halfway along when I realise that the blue in the distance isn't just sky, but ocean.

'Oh, wow!' Bex says. She breaks into a little skippy-hop run, but then stops and turns back to us. 'We're so close!' She's beaming.

'Yep. Just a couple of blocks,' Oscar says.

'Wow!' Bex says again. She walks alongside

us, but I can tell she just wants to run ahead and, knowing her, jump straight into the water.

I realise Oscar and I have actually started to speed up too and the image of us all just running into the ocean makes me grin. We emerge onto a promenade separated from the beach by a strip of grass. Oscar stops and holds one finger up as if he's about to make an announcement. Bex and I stare at him, dutifully.

'Now this is Ocean Front Walk,' he says. 'Very important. It's where I work, but apart from that there are shops and cafés and it's where you'll find the Venice Art Crawl. Basically, a lot of stuff happens here.'

Bex and I nod and then I say, 'Can we go on the beach now?'

He grins and bends down to take off his shoes. Bex squees – really, she actually says 'Squee!' – and runs off across the sand.

'They grow up so fast,' Oscar jokes, smiling after her.

I kick off my flip-flops and am surprised to find that, despite the sun, the sand is actually quite cool. We follow Bex down towards the water.

I walk in till the freezing water's up to my knees and let it swirl around me, as a group of large birds – pelicans, I think – fly past, skimming the sparkling surf.

'I can't believe we live here!' Bex shouts.

I was just thinking the same thing.

Chapter Seven

We walk a little way along the beach in front of a huge sand dune that Oscar tells us is man-made – some little kids are trying to slide down it on plastic bin lids, but they're not having much success – and then Oscar says he's going to show us where he works. Apparently he's got two jobs, but he won't tell us what they are yet.

He tells us that Ocean Front Walk is known as 'the Boardwalk' along this stretch. It's an outrageous place – I've never been anywhere quite like it. Stalls selling T-shirts, friendship bracelets and other tourist tat stand opposite shops offering tattoos, 'medical marijuana', oxygen facials or 'Botox on the

Beach'. We can smell the weed, along with incense, fried onions and coffee.

We pass the famous Muscle Beach, which I'd always thought was just a bit of the beach where people worked out, but it's actually a sort of concrete outdoor gym. Disappointingly, there's only one guy working out there: he has enormous muscles and an equally enormous afro. In front of the 'Freak Show' a man tells a small crowd, 'We've got a dog in there, but it's got five legs. Sorry, kids!'

When Bex and I aren't looking at the buildings – loads of which feature bright murals – we're looking at the people. The dazed-looking tourists are outnumbered by skateboarders, buskers, guys selling CDs of their own music, which Oscar tells us they will insist on signing with your name therefore ensuring you buy one, and homeless people with cardboard signs reading things like HONESTLY HUNGRY.

There's so much to look at, and it's so different from home, that it's hard to take it all in. I take loads of photos on my phone before realising that we live here now and I really don't need to fill up my memory card with stuff I can see every day.

After walking for maybe ten minutes – some of it on the Boardwalk and some back on the beach, which Bex just can't resist – we come to a small, brown wooden building designed to look like a boat.

Oscar stops and says, 'Ta-da.'

It's a noodle bar. Called Wok the Boat.

'Wok the Boat?' I say, grinning. 'Seriously?'

'I know,' Oscar says. 'Fantastic, isn't it?'

I pull a face and he laughs and ushers me and Bex inside. As we walk in, a shout of 'Oscar!' goes up from staff and, I think, customers.

'So they know you here?' I joke.

He grins at me. 'Home from home.'

Inside it's also designed to look like a boat, with panelled walls, portholes, rigging hanging from the ceiling. I can even hear seagulls and ocean sounds, which I assume are recorded, but could possibly be real (we're on the beach, after all).

Oscar introduces us to the girl behind the counter (the front of which is covered with embedded shells and pebbles). Her name is Tabby and she looks about the same age as me, maybe a bit older, with dark, bobbed hair, bright blue eyes, and a perfect

Cupid's bow mouth. She looks like a silent-movie star.

'So you're the famous Emma,' she says. It could be my imagination, but I think she sneers a little. She's got a stack of cardboard in front of her and she folds a sheet into those little takeaway boxes I've only ever seen on American TV and films as she talks. She does it so quickly, I can't even tell what she's doing until it's done.

'Famous for what?' I ask.

'Oscar's been telling us all about you,' she says, and I notice she's got a gap between her two front teeth. 'He's been real excited about having a friend from home.'

She stops folding long enough to reach over and ruffle Oscar's hair. He pulls away, but he's laughing.

'I haven't talked about you that much,' he tells me.

'Really?' Tabby says, and raises one eyebrow. 'How much has Oscar talked about Emma?' she says.

I don't see who she's talking to, but I hear a male voice say, 'Emma? Emma from England? Emma he's known since he was a child? Emma who went to New York? Emma who he went to see *Gladiator* with, even though they were too young, and she fell asleep? That Emma? Or a different one?'

'Shut up,' says Oscar. He's grinning, but his cheeks are patchy and red.

The owner of the voice appears – it's a really tall black guy, who also reaches over and ruffles Oscar's hair.

'Hi,' he says to me. 'I'm Sam. And you are?' He grins.

I reach over and shake his hand. 'And this is Bex,' I tell him, pulling my sister alongside me.

Sam says, 'Oh, don't worry! We've heard about you too.'

Bex almost preens, which makes me laugh.

'You hungry?' Oscar asks me and Bex. We both nod. 'Should I order for you?' he asks and we nod again.

He says something that sounds like, 'Three two-one-sixes and a robot on the side' and then looks at us for approval. Since I have no idea what he asked for and nor, presumably, does Bex, we both just nod again. We're starting to look like those little nodding dogs you sometimes see on the back shelves of cars.

Sam heads over to the massive stove – the kitchen is open to the rest of the place – and starts throwing things in an enormous wok. And then he starts singing. It takes me a second to work out what it is, but then I realise it's 'Firework' by Katy Perry. I grin.

'He's a big pop fan,' Tabby says, without even looking up from her box-folding. 'It's charming at first...'

'You want to sit outside?' Oscar asks and, rather than nodding, Bex and I just turn towards the door.

Sam is still singing and Tabby's still folding as the door swings shut behind us.

We sit down at a tiny table right on the sand and I find myself staring out over the water again. The sun is glittering off the waves and it's just so lovely to be sitting outside and be warm. Even though it's summer, it was raining when we left Manchester, and if the past few years have been anything to go by, it probably would have continued that way until November, when the snow arrived.

'How long have you worked here?' Bex asks Oscar, as I'm still looking out to sea and daydreaming.

'A while now,' Oscar says. 'I worked at a Taco Bell

first and I hated that, but then Tabby left to come here and she recruited me. We have a really good laugh together and the owner leaves us to our own devices most of the time, so it's much more flexible and relaxed. Are you going to be looking for a job?' he asks me. 'Because we're always looking for staff.'

I shake my head. 'I don't know. Honestly, I haven't even thought about it yet. I probably will, yeah, but...' I don't want to say 'I don't want to work in a restaurant' so I just let the sentence drift off.

Sam comes out with little takeaway boxes and puts them down on the table along with a jug of water (with lemon slices) and three glasses. 'Enjoy!' he says, and goes back inside almost before we can say thank you.

'I've always wanted to eat out of one of these boxes,' I say to no one in particular, as I open the lid and the steam practically fogs my eyeballs.

'Careful,' Oscar says. 'It's hot.'

My snort of laughter blows some steam away and reveals that the box contains noodles and chopped peanuts.

'What is this?' I ask him.

'Pad thai. Just wait and then taste it. It's amazing.'

'Have you got the same?'

He nods as he opens the box Sam put in the middle. 'And these are spring rolls. But amazing spring rolls. Just wait—'

I reach into the box and then yank my hand out.

'—until they cool down,' Oscar says.

I poke at my noodles, but they're too hot as well.

'Does this place do well?' I ask Oscar, glancing back at the facade. I notice SINCE 1988 on the sign.

Oscar nods. 'They're talking about opening another one. Guess the name.'

'We Will Wok You?' I try.

'That's terrible!' Bex says.

'And Wok the Boat isn't?'

'Wok 'n' Roll,' Bex says.

'Oh!' Oscar says, almost leaping out of his seat. 'It could be a bowling alley theme!'

Bex and I both squint at him and I say, 'Oh dear.'

'Yeah,' he says, grinning. 'Sorry about that.'

Bex wrinkles her nose. 'Wok-a-bye-baby? It could have a crèche...'

'The Wok Ness Monster,' Oscar says. 'Scottish themed.'

'Wok DJ!' I almost shout.

'That one might actually work,' Oscar says, grinning. 'Here's a hint: it's open twenty-four hours...'

'Wok the Night?' I try.

'Wok *All* Night!' Bex says.

'Wok Around the Clock,' Oscar says. 'Brilliant, no?'

I laugh and then dig in to my noodles. They're still slightly too hot – they make me gasp out little puffs of steam – but they taste amazing. Soft and crunchy and sweet and sour all at the same time.

Once we've finished the fabulous noodles and eaten the best spring rolls in the world, *ever* (Oscar was right about that), we go inside to say bye to Tabby and Sam and then walk towards Santa Monica Pier, which we've been able to see in the distance since we first set off from Venice.

In New York last summer, Jessie and I kept finding it disorientating seeing places that were incredibly familiar from films. It's the same here. Walking towards Santa Monica Pier, looking back at the houses along the oceanfront, gives me a ridiculous sense of déjà vu.

'What film would I have seen this in?' I ask Oscar.

'I was just thinking that,' Bex says. 'It's so familiar.'

'Did you ever watch *The OC*?' Oscar asks. 'They filmed here a bit, I think. Loads of films and TV shows have filmed here. Music videos too. I can't think...' He scrunches up his face, trying to remember.

'Oh!' Bex says, suddenly. '*The Hannah Montana Movie*!'

Oscar and I burst out laughing and Bex goes a bit red. 'I know...'

'I can't believe it took you even that long to remember that,' I say. 'Didn't you used to watch it every day?'

'Not *every* day,' she says, smiling.

'You did,' I say. 'Actually, Dad once heard a noise in the middle of the night, thought we were being burgled, went downstairs and found Bex watching *Hannah Montana*!'

'Don't worry, Bex,' Oscar says. 'We all love Miley Cyrus.'

Bex laughs. 'I don't watch it any more.'

'I bet you really want to now though, don't you?' Oscar says.

'I do actually...' Bex grins.

'Emma said you've got an audition lined up?' Oscar asks Bex.

'No, not an audition, just a meeting, but if it goes well I'll be going to some castings. I hope.'

We climb some steps off the main promenade, up to the actual pier. A group of tourists are taking it in turns to have their picture taken under the blue WORLD FAMOUS SANTA MONICA PIER sign.

As we walk through the car park, Bex tells Oscar about Starmakers and all the productions she's been involved in. Then she breaks off to say, 'It smells like the seaside here!'

And she's right, it does. Like salt and sun cream, popcorn and candyfloss. It reminds me of the resorts we used to go to as kids, like Blackpool, Southport and Lytham St Annes. Once, Mum and Dad picked us up from school and took us straight to St Annes as a surprise. It was a really hot day and we sang along with the radio in the car and stopped for fish and chips at the pier, then we sat on the sand dunes and watched the sun set. Mum, Bex and I all fell asleep on the way home. Dad complained, but he didn't really mind.

I feel my eyes start to prickle so I squeeze them closed and, when I open them, we're passing a man wearing an eye-patch and carrying a parrot on his shoulder. I blink.

'He's here every single time I come,' Oscar tells us once we're out of the man's earshot. 'He's had that parrot for fifty years, he told me once.'

We walk along the outside of the pier, past a row of booths, each one hosting a children's party. Music and balloons drift out onto the boardwalk. Once we've passed them all, I stop and look out across the beach and ocean, back towards Venice. The beach is wide and the sand pale. The sky is pure blue without a single cloud. The blue of the ocean reflects the sky and white waves roll in as far as I can see.

'Isn't it gorgeous?' Bex says.

I nod. It really is.

'I thought we'd go on the Ferris wheel, for the best view,' Oscar says. 'You up for it?'

We walk to the end of the pier and look up at the wheel, all red and yellow against the bright blue of the sky.

'I don't like heights,' I say.

'Oh, come on!' Bex says. 'We'll be with you, you'll be fine.'

It does look really beautiful and the view will be incredible, I'm sure.

'Please?' Bex says, squeezing my arm and doing this stupid puppy face she's done since she was practically a toddler.

I laugh. 'OK. But if I faint or wet myself, you've only yourselves to blame.'

In the queue for the wheel, we're made to hop up on stools and pose for a photo. It's in a little wooden shelter, like a bus shelter, so I don't know what that's about. While we wait, Oscar remembers a few more films and TV shows the pier's been in, but they're all crime or gangster things neither Bex nor I have seen. We get to the front of the queue, scan our tickets in a little machine, and then climb in. The wheel doesn't have the usual little swinging carriage seats; it has round gondolas with umbrellas over the top, which means we can all get in the same one. My stomach wobbles as we get in and the whole thing moves, but I feel better once I'm sitting down.

It lifts and slowly climbs until we can see back along the Boardwalk, out to the ocean and even further back, across beautiful houses and to distant hills.

'Is that the Hollywood Hills?' Bex asks Oscar.

He nods. 'Are you free tomorrow? I could give you the grand tour. There's a bus tour – it's a bit touristy, but it's a good overview.'

'We can go, can't we?' Bex asks me.

I nod, but I must look a bit pained – or she notices that I'm clutching the edge of the plastic seat – because she asks if I'm all right.

And I am. The only bit I can't cope with is when we go over the top and, for a second, I can't see the wheel, just the ocean and the sky. It makes me feel like I could float away. I don't like it.

We sit in silence for a while, taking it all in, and the next time we get to the top I stare at my feet until my eyes blur.

'You're not working tomorrow?' Bex asks Oscar.

'I'm working in the evening.'

'And what about your other job? What's that?' I ask him.

Oscar taps his nose. 'All in good time.'

I roll my eyes.

Bex laughs. 'Are you a strippergram?'

'Yes,' Oscar says, his face serious. 'The ladies pay a lot of money to see my...stuff.'

And then he blushes. I knew he hadn't changed that much. His 'stuff' indeed.

I take a few photos on my phone and text them to Jessie and then the ride's finished. As we leave, we're offered the photograph taken in the booth as we queued. The bus-shelter background has been replaced with a photo of the view from the wheel, to make it look as if the picture was actually taken on the wheel itself. Despite our protests, Oscar buys one.

'You should always buy the cheesy memento,' Oscar says. 'The crappier the better.'

We walk back down the pier, looking at the bowling and shooting games where you can win giant Angry Birds, and inhaling the caramel smell from the popcorn carts.

'Do you want to do any other rides?' Oscar asks. 'Or is that enough for today?'

'I think that'll do me,' I say. 'Bex?'

'I think I might just go and lie on the deck or the roof,' Bex says. 'I want to email some friends and Dad.'

'Right,' I say. I have no plans to email Dad, but it would probably be nice to spend a bit of time with Mum before she starts work in the morning.

'Do you want to come back with us?' I ask Oscar.

He shakes his head. 'Thanks for asking, but, no, I've got some stuff I need to do. I'll pick you up tomorrow about eleven, though, OK?'

We walk back along the Boardwalk, dodging cyclists, tandems and people actually rollerblading. It looks so much like I imagined before we left Manchester that I look down at my chest to make sure my boobs haven't magically inflated. (They haven't.)

Chapter Eight

My sister wakes me up by practically yelling the words, 'You have to promise to say yes!'

'Whaa?' I mumble, rolling over and pulling the duvet – comforter, whatever – over my face.

'You have to promise to say yes!' she says again.

'I'm not promising anything until I know what you're talking about,' I say from under the covers.

'That's exactly my point. You have to. This is the most important thing that's ever happened to me and you have to—'

'Promise to say yes. Yeah. I got that. What is it?' I shuffle up the bed and rest against my pillows while Bex bounces up and down at the foot of the bed. I try opening one eye, but my room is so bright that I close it again instantly.

'Promise!' Bex says.

'Oh, for god's sake,' I say. 'I promise. But I've got my fingers crossed. Now tell me.'

'Emily wants to see me to discuss a casting,' she says, and throws herself down on the bed next to me.

I open my eyes and squint at her. 'Seriously?'

Emily is Emily Hennigar, the agent friend of Vivienne's from Starmakers.

'*Yes!* Today! There's something she thinks I'd be perfect for and she wants to see me today at twelve. Mum's going to meet us there, cos you have to have a parent with you—'

'Wait. What time is it? Has Mum gone already?'

'Yes! It's ten o'clock. She left at nine. She says she can meet us, but you have to stay with me until Mum gets there. There isn't anyone else!'

'Well now that you've made me feel so special, I don't see how I can say no.'

'*Oh my god!*' Bex shrieks, right next to my ear. She grabs me and squeezes me then runs out of the room, chuntering to herself about what she's going to wear.

I pull the duvet back over my head. I can't believe my little sister's got a meeting with a Hollywood agent on practically our first day here. I know Vivienne said Emily was keen, but I didn't expect this. I shouldn't really be surprised, though, I've always known Bex was determined – from the minute she convinced Mum and Dad to send her to Starmakers she's been really serious about it all. She's had a lot to fit in around school, but they insisted that her schoolwork didn't suffer and so she's worked really hard to make sure nothing slipped. And she honestly is good. I didn't know what to expect the first time I saw her performing – I knew she was dramatic, but that doesn't necessarily translate – but she's great. Offstage she's sweet and funny, but a bit of a doofus; onstage she sort of glows. She's got charisma, I suppose.

'How are we going to get there?' I ask Bex. I'm now out of bed, showered and dressed and sitting on the terrace. Bex is sitting cross-legged on the floor, eyes closed, trying to 'centre' herself. I'm sitting at the table with a gigantic mug of coffee and a plate of toast with peanut butter.

'Mum suggested Oscar might be able to drive us,' Bex says. 'Since he was going to be spending the day with us anyway. Can you ring him?'

'Has he even got a car? He didn't mention one.'

'Mum says Michael says he has. Can you just phone him and ask him?'

'Certainly, miss,' I say, standing up and pretending to curtsey, even though her eyes are still closed so she won't appreciate the sarcasm.

I get my phone from my bedroom and ring Oscar.

'Have you got a car?' I say, when he answers.

'Sort of,' he says. 'Why?'

I tell him about Bex's audition and he says driving us is no problem.

'Will we still be able to do the grand tour tomorrow?' I ask him.

'Oh, I think I can manage that. Wouldn't want you to miss out.'

I smile. 'I'm concerned about the "sort of" car. How can you sort of have a car?'

'You'll know when you see it,' he says. 'Where's the agent's office? Somewhere fancy?'

I take the phone outside and ask Bex, who is now doing the downward dog.

'Wilshire Boulevard,' she says from between her legs.

I tell Oscar.

'Oh. Not fancy at all, then,' he says, and laughs. 'I'll just have to let you out and park elsewhere. Somewhere the parking doesn't cost more than the car's worth.'

We confirm the rest of the details and then I go back to my breakfast while Bex finishes up her yoga by lying flat on her back and humming gently to herself. It's really amazing that we're even related.

I sit with my face turned up to the sun and Bex comes outside every now and then in a different outfit and says, 'What do you think?' before saying 'No. I know,' and leaving again before I've even had a chance to comment. Eventually she comes out wearing a denim skirt, red-and-white-striped T-shirt and brogues.

'That looks great,' I tell her, before she has a chance to reject it. 'Simple, effortless, chic. Age-appropriate. The brogues make it quirky, but not too quirky. Perfect.'

'Do you really think so?' she asks, looking down at her shoes.

'I really do,' I say. 'You should leave your hair down too. It looks great.'

'And natural make-up, right?'

'As little as possible,' I tell her. 'She'll want to see your face.'

While Bex was changing, I googled Emily Hennigar and was surprised to find both that she's English – she went to the same posh girls' school as Clare, Dad's new girlfriend – and she's pretty young. She looks like she's in her early thirties. But she's definitely a successful and professional agent. She discovered Leanne Carr, the star of that sci-fi film where the kids get trapped in their school by aliens, and she also represents Cate Cooke from that Disney series about the boring daughter of the out-of-control rockstar couple.

I'm emailing Jessie some of the photos I took

yesterday when Bex comes back out to the terrace and says, 'Didn't you hear the door? Oscar's here.'

I step into my ballet pumps and follow her downstairs and outside where Oscar is standing next to the most pathetic-looking car I think I've ever seen.

'Your chariot awaits, madam,' he says, bowing to Bex, who giggles like it's the most charming-looking car she's ever seen.

'Does this even go?' I ask, walking around to look at the back of the car. It's an old VW Beetle. It's white, but so dappled with patches of rust that it looks a bit like a giraffe.

Oscar tuts at me. 'Of course it goes! It got me here, didn't it?'

'You live about two streets away,' I say.

'Yes! And it only took me half an hour,' he says, joking. At least, I hope he's joking.

'Were you pushing it?' I ask, one eyebrow raised.

'For that,' he says, 'you're sitting in the back.' He opens the passenger door and gestures at me to climb over into the back. Of course. It's only a two-door. Tragic. I clamber over, catching my skirt on a jagged bit of metal at the side of the door. I reach back and pull it free, hoping I haven't just shown Oscar my knickers. I glance over my shoulder and the look on his face suggests both that I have and that he may have liked whatever it was he saw. I flop down on the back seat, which is covered in cracked plastic and sags in the middle, and put my hands up to my face. How embarrassing.

'Make yourself comfortable,' Oscar mumbles, then yanks the front seat back again so that Bex can get in.

'Isn't this great?' Bex says, looking over her shoulder at me.

'Wonderful,' I say, trying to find somewhere to put my legs. I end up with one foot in each footwell and reach round for the seatbelt.

Oscar gets in and slams his door.

'Are we ready?' he says, looking at me in the rear-view mirror.

'I don't know,' Bex says. 'I think I might be sick.'

'Well, that window doesn't open,' Oscar says,

cheerfully, 'so if you are going to spew, you'll have to open the door. Put your seatbelt on. Wouldn't want you falling out.'

Bex laughs and I boggle at both of them. This is LA. And we're heading out in a total death trap.

'Are you really nervous?' Oscar asks Bex as he reverses down the road at the back of our house.

He's got one arm over the back of Bex's seat so he can look over his shoulder and I feel slightly embarrassed that I'm sitting there in the middle of his reverse view. I slide down a bit in my seat. Oscar's wearing a relatively normal outfit today: skinny jeans – except they're bright green, so he looks a bit like a poppy – and a black, short-sleeved T-shirt, and I can see the muscles flexing in his arm as he manoeuvres the car. I would never have imagined that Oscar had muscles in his arms or anywhere else. Combined with the fact that he's actually driving, well...it's distracting.

'I'm a bit nervous,' Bex says, and I force myself to look at the back of her head instead. 'It keeps coming in waves. One minute I feel really calm – like this is meant to be – and the next thing I know I think

I'm going to throw up and I just want to forget the whole idea.'

'I'm sure she's nice, this Emily woman,' I tell her. 'Vivienne wouldn't have recommended her if she wasn't.'

'She did say she's nice. But how nice can you be if you're a successful Hollywood agent? I just wish this wasn't my first time doing this kind of thing.'

'There's something to be said for being thrown in at the deep end, though,' Oscar says. 'Also for starting at the top.'

Bex nods. 'That's what Vivienne says too. But I'd feel better if I knew what to expect. I've googled it, but it all depends on the agent, I think.'

'I think you'll be fantastic,' Oscar says. 'You're clearly talented. You're confident. You look adorable. I think they'll snap you up.'

Bex giggles and preens and says, 'Thank you, Oscar!'

That's the kind of thing I should have said to her, I realise now, but it honestly didn't occur to me. Oscar seems to be able to think of the right thing to say at the right time. I never think of the right thing to say until the moment's long gone. Oscar used to be like that too – what happened?

Oscar reverses out into the road, only having to stop three times when other drivers honk at him. Finally we make it out and Oscar says, 'Now. Which way, I wonder...' But he's joking.

He heads off down the main street – South Venice Boulevard, he tells us – and drives for a while along the wide, straight road while Bex talks about Cate Cooke's TV show and tells Oscar how Emily Hennigar discovered Leanne Carr and how her career's gone stratospheric since the sci-fi film.

I stare out of the window, feeling a bit disorientated. LA's not at all like I expected. This street is wide, but sort of friendly looking with trees along each side and, in some places, down the middle. It's also lined with a huge variety of buildings, from shops to office blocks, to family houses with children's toys in the garden. Even the buses are cool – red and silver with bike racks on the front. It makes Manchester seem claustrophobic somehow. I think back to last summer in New York and it seems cramped and too busy in comparison.

Bex has moved on to asking Oscar about learning to drive. He learned here at school.

'You start Drivers' Ed in ninth grade here, so that's when you're fifteen,' he says.

'I'm starting eighth grade in September,' Bex says. 'They're seriously going to teach me to drive in a couple of years' time?'

'I doubt it,' I tell her. 'I think they'll make an exception for you.'

Bex turns round and sticks her tongue out at me.

'And you,' she says. 'You'll be learning to drive too.'

'At school? But I'll have missed Drivers' Ed. I don't know – learning to drive is scary enough without doing it in a foreign country.'

'It's not a foreign country, though,' Bex says. 'Not now we live here.'

I roll my eyes. It's not like it's permanent. If things don't work out with Mum at the university, we could be back in Manchester in a few months. Excuse me if I don't get too invested in being here.

After about twenty minutes, we pull onto the highway and I find myself sitting up straighter, as if my vigilance can keep this car on the road. The road is rough – like it's being resurfaced – and Oscar's car is vibrating and making an odd high-pitched humming sound.

'It's not so comfy on the highways, I'll admit,' Oscar says, crossing about five lanes completely casually.

Apart from the vibrating and the odd noise, it's actually not so bad driving on the highway at all. Oscar seems completely confident which, despite the ridiculousness of the car, makes me feel confident too. And obviously Bex feels the same since she's barely paused for breath the whole way here. Oscar gets off the highway just as easily as he got on it and then we're on another wide tree-lined street, but the buildings are bigger and shinier and it's clear we're heading downtown. We drive for a while longer, and then turn right into a cleaner, more expensive-looking street.

'This is it, Wilshire Boulevard,' Oscar says. 'I looked on Google Maps and I think the office is pretty near the Beverly Wilshire...' Oscar slows down, peering out of the windscreen. 'So it should be somewhere along here.' He suddenly swings the car off the main road and down a side street, which I'm really surprised to see looks residential.

'I just remembered I parked here once before,' Oscar says, 'when Mum came and we went to Rodeo Drive. There's free parking if you can find a space. It's a lot better than one of the parking lots.'

The street is actually really lovely with gorgeous houses with big gardens out in front. Oscar parks between two expensive-looking cars and says, 'There goes the neighbourhood.'

On Wilshire, we find the building we need – it's a rather boring-looking beige block with black windows – and wait for Mum, but by five to twelve she still hasn't arrived and Bex is starting to panic. I've tried her mobile, but it's just ringing.

'OK,' I tell my sister, 'we'll go up. Me and you. And we'll tell her that Mum's on her way. Better that than Emily thinking we haven't turned up.'

Bex nods. Her eyes are really wide and I can tell she's nervous. Obviously standing out here's not helping.

Oscar tells us he'll wait for us in the car and

we thank him, before I push open the double glass doors to the building and usher my sister inside.

The reception area is very quiet, very cream and very empty. The only furniture is a huge marble desk with a rather snooty-looking blonde woman sitting behind it.

We announce ourselves and the receptionist adjusts her headset, presses a button on her phone and then says, 'You can go up – third floor.'

As we walk past the receptionist to the lifts, Bex grabs my hand, squeezes and then drops it. I smile at her. I want to say something, but it's too quiet here.

As soon as the lift doors close and I've pressed the button for the third floor, I say, 'You'll be fine. Don't worry.'

'I just wish Mum was here,' she says, and then pulls a face. 'I don't mean I'm not glad you're here, but Emily won't let me audition without Mum.'

'She'll get here,' I tell her.

The lift doors open and we step out onto the third floor and into some surprisingly deep carpet – it feels like I'm walking on sponge. The receptionist here is also blonde, but much less snooty. She smiles at us, at least, which is more than the downstairs one did.

'I'm Bex Robinson?' Bex says, surprising me. Even though her voice does the questioning thing at the end, she sounds confident.

'Of course,' the receptionist says. 'Emily's on a call right now, but she should be free soon. Would you like to take a seat?'

Bex nods and starts to turn towards the seats, but turns back again and says, 'This is my sister, Emma. My mum is on her way, but she must have been held up...'

'Don't worry,' the receptionist says. She's still smiling. 'She's probably stuck in traffic.'

We sit down on one of the huge leather sofas and I check my phone in case there's a text from Mum. There isn't.

Bex flicks through a copy of *Variety*, while I stare at the plain white wall and try to will Mum here with the force of my mind. We've been sitting here for about five minutes, when the door to what I assume is Emily's office opens and then Emily herself pops her head out and smiles at us both.

'Bex?' she says, brightly. She looks even younger in real life than she did online. She's very pretty and blonde and she's wearing a bright white shirt over a pink pencil skirt.

Bex drops the magazine on the floor and starts struggling to her feet, while simultaneously apologising for, I assume, not being poised in a state of cat-like readiness for Emily's appearance.

'Don't panic,' Emily says, smiling. She looks at me. 'You're not Bex's mum!'

I smile. 'No. I'm her sister, Emma. Mum is—'

There's a ping from the lift and Emily says, 'Here, I think! What excellent timing!'

We all wait to see who emerges from the lift and, thank goodness, it is Mum. She looks slightly flustered and immediately starts apologising, saying she was stuck in traffic and her phone was playing up.

'Oh, the traffic,' Emily says. 'It takes some getting used to, I know that.'

I'm standing up as well by this point and the four of us all just look at each other for a moment, before Emily says, 'Well, come in!' and disappears back into her office. She's still talking as she goes, apologising to Mum about dragging her away from her first day at work.

Emily's office is huge, with three windows overlooking Wilshire Boulevard. Framed film and TV posters cover the other three walls. Emily sits down at her white desk, with its shiny silver Mac, gigantic bunch of shocking-pink flowers and neat pile of scripts, and gestures at us to sit on leather sofas that look much the same as those outside. Mum sits next to Bex and I sit on the opposite sofa.

'I've just been looking at your showreel,' Emily says, from behind her desk. 'It's absolutely wonderful.'

'Thank you,' Bex says.

'Vivienne is wild about you. She was disappointed to lose you, I know that. But her loss is my gain!'

We all laugh politely. Emily comes out from behind her desk and perches on the sofa next to me, but she leans her elbows on her knees and looks intently at Bex.

'So, I've literally just found out that the part I was going to send you out for – the reason I wanted you here at such short notice – has been cast.' She rolls her eyes. 'It's gone to Debby Ryan – they've decided to go older. I still want to send you out to see a few people, but now that we've got a bit of time, I want to do some work with you here first – work on some audition pieces, make sure you know exactly what you're doing. It helps that—'

The phone rings and Emily says, 'Excuse me' and heads back to her desk.

I look at my sister, who looks absolutely transfixed. I mouth 'Are you OK?' at her, and she nods.

'Oh, send him in!' Emily says.

I glance over my shoulder at her – send who in? – and then the door opens and my question is answered.

It's Alex Hall. He's the star of a TV show called *Stellar Highway* that hasn't even been shown in the UK yet, but he's all over every celebrity magazine and gossip website, thanks to rumours of flings with Cate Cooke and a pre-Bieber Selena Gomez. And then there's an advert he did for jeans, which left very little to the imagination.

'Alex!' Emily says, crossing the room to the door and giving him three air kisses.

He glances over at us and smiles. I look at my sister – her mouth is hanging open. I realise mine is too and I close it.

'I was just passing,' Alex says. 'So I thought I'd come and pick up the—'

'Oh yes, of course!' Emily says. Then she leans out of the door. 'Genevieve? Could you gather Alex's fan mail? Thanks, darling.'

'Have you got five minutes?' she asks Alex. 'I'd love you to meet Bex Robinson.'

Alex comes over and smiles at the three of us. He's actually even more gorgeous than he looks in photos. His dark hair is short, but with a floppy fringe that hangs in his eyes. I've only ever seen him clean-shaven in photos, but he's got a bit of stubble and it suits him – along with the bridge of his nose being just a little bit crooked, it stops him looking too perfect. And he smells amazing.

Emily introduces us and he shakes our hands. His hand is warm. And soft.

'Could you do a quick reading with Bex?' Emily asks him. 'I'm going to start sending her out, but I want to give her a bit of boot camp first, so reading with you would be perfect.'

Alex grins. 'No problem.'

'Great!' Emily says. She's halfway back to her desk, before she turns and says, 'That's OK with you, Bex?'

'Of course,' Bex says, and again she sounds incredibly confident. I'm so impressed.

Alex sits next to me, hitching his jeans up a bit as he does. I shuffle in my seat so I'm turned slightly towards him. Emily hands him and Bex a script each and I ask her, 'Should I move?'

She shakes her head. 'You're fine where you are, sweetheart. Bex? If you just start where I've highlighted? Feel free to stop if you need to. No pressure.'

Bex nods and I notice she's chewing her lip a bit so I know she's nervous, but you wouldn't know it when she starts to read. I don't recognise the script at all, but it's a pretty snappy back and forth conversation between her and Alex.

Bex pauses or stumbles a couple of times, but each time she recovers and doesn't seem to let it bother her. Alex is totally confident and I can see why he became so famous, so fast. He's leaning back in his seat, very relaxed, but giving a completely convincing reading. Plus his slight Southern accent is very sexy.

I'm actually disappointed when Emily stops them.

'Well, that was fantastic,' she says. 'Really wonderful.'

'You're very good,' Alex tells Bex.

She blushes and grins and I feel so incredibly proud of her.

'You know what else I think would be useful, Alex?' Emily says. 'If Bex came down to the show and had a bit of a nosy around. She's never been on a set before – that's right isn't it, sweetheart?'

Bex nods.

'Could Jordan show her the ropes?' she asks Alex.

Alex nods. 'You can see the set, take the tour. You'll love it.'

'Great,' Emily says. 'So we'll get that set up ASAP.'

We all just sit there, smiling at each other for a second and then Alex says, 'So I'll just see Genevieve?'

'Absolutely!' Emily says. 'I'm sure she's got that ready for you now.'

As Alex stands up, his leg brushes against mine and sends tingles reverberating through my entire body.

'I'll call Jordan and set everything up,' Emily tells him.

'Lovely to meet you,' Mum says.

'You too,' he says, smiling. 'And I'll see you at the studio,' he says to Bex. And then he leaves. His back view is just as good as the front view and he's wearing the jeans he advertised. That advert was so popular that I bet they gave him a lifetime's supply.

As soon as Emily closes the door behind him, she turns and grins at us. 'That was a stroke of luck! Alex's PA, Jordan, will look after you – he's absolutely lovely. It will be really useful for you to see the studios and have a look behind the scenes of a TV show.'

'It sounds fantastic,' Bex says. 'Thank you so much.'

'There's a lot of work ahead,' Emily says. 'But

I've got a good feeling about you. It helps that you're English – everyone's looking for the next Keira Knightley or Carey Mulligan.'

For the next five minutes Emily tells Mum what she has planned for Bex – she wants to film Bex doing some test auditions and she also wants Bex to practise filming herself on the computer; apparently quite a lot of auditions are done on video these days. If I can't bring her to Emily's office, Emily will send a car, but Mum will need to accompany Bex to any auditions Emily arranges.

As we leave, she says, 'Bex Robinson? Are you a Rebecca? How do you feel about Rebecca Robinson?'

'That's...fine,' Bex says.

Three minutes later, we're back out on Wilshire Boulevard, slightly dazed and blinking in the sunshine.

Chapter Nine

When we get back to Venice, we take Oscar to lunch to thank him for driving us to Emily's office and back.

He suggests we go to the Sidewalk Café, which Oscar says is a Venice Beach institution. We sit outside under the awning, next to the Boardwalk. Just in front of the café, a small crowd has gathered to watch a guy who's playing guitar directly opposite us.

A waiter comes to take our drink order – all three of us get Cokes – and then, as we're watching the guitarist, a bunch of people go past on Segways.

'Segways!' I shriek and point. Not cool. But I've never seen one in real life before.

'Oh yeah,' Oscar says. 'You can do Segway tours of Venice and Santa Monica. They go past a lot, looking like dorks.'

I laugh. Growing up, Oscar was the biggest dork I knew. By far.

'It wouldn't be so bad if they didn't have to wear helmets,' he says, and I grin at him.

He knew he was a dork. He was totally fine with it too. It used to bug me a bit – why didn't he want to be cool? I desperately wanted to be cool – didn't everyone? But, no, Oscar was comfortable with his nerdiness. And he certainly seems to have embraced it now. Maybe this is the perfect place for that kind of thing.

'We should go on the tour!' Bex says.

'I don't know about that,' Oscar says. 'I've got my street cred to think about.'

'I think if you're referring to it as "street cred", that ship's sailed,' I say.

The waiter brings out Cokes and takes our food order. I get a cheeseburger and Bex gets a turkey burger, but Oscar goes for one with all sorts of extra stuff – avocado and bacon and various cheeses.

'You've done right to start basic, though,' he tells me. 'There's plenty of time to work up to my level.'

I roll my eyes and sip my Coke.

The guitarist is now playing his guitar behind his back, so we watch him for a while.

'Some people are so talented,' I say.

'You're talented!' Oscar says, sounding shocked.

'Me?' I say. 'Bex is. But I'm not.'

'You are!' Oscar says. 'Your drawings were fantastic. I've still got a couple of them.'

I laugh. 'Have you? Thanks. But I'm only OK at drawing. He's properly talented.'

The guitarist is still playing with his guitar behind his back.

'That's just showing off,' Oscar jokes.

'Your drawings are amazing,' Bex says, nodding. 'I've kept loads of them too. So have Mum and Dad.'

'Seriously?' I ask her. 'I had no idea.'

'You don't draw any more?' Oscar asks.

I shake my head. 'Not really.'

'You did that Empire State Building for Jessie,' Bex says. 'It was fantastic.'

'That was just because we saw it looking like

a pencil drawing when we were in New York, so...
I haven't done anything else for ages.'

'Why not?' Oscar asks.

'I don't know. I just got out of the habit, I suppose.'

'That's not what Dad said,' Bex says, frowning.

I narrow my eyes at her. 'What did Dad say?'

'He said...' she starts and then stops. 'Actually, I think he said I shouldn't mention it to you.'

'Bit late for that now,' I say, gulping some Coke to prepare myself.

'Well, it's not like it's something really bad,' she says. 'He said you give up on things too easily. If you're not good at something – or successful at it, maybe it was – straight away, then you give up.'

I stare at her. 'I don't think that's true,' I say. And it's a bit rich coming from him – I'm not the one who gave up on our family, am I?

'Well, I wasn't sure at first,' Bex says, 'but when I thought about it, I think he's right. That course you were going to do at the art college? What happened there?'

'The tutor told me he didn't think my work was original enough,' I say.

'But you could've gone anyway and proved him wrong,' Bex says. 'You just decided not to go.'

I nod. 'But why would I waste my time with someone who didn't believe in me? I needed encouragement and I obviously wasn't going to get it from him.'

'Unless it was a test,' Oscar said. 'Unless he says that to everyone to test how dedicated they are.'

I stare at him. 'So I failed.'

He shrugs. 'I just think people will try to put you off doing what you want to do – I don't know why they do that, but they definitely do – but if you really want something you have to ignore everyone else and do it anyway. And I know you could be an amazing artist, but you're not planning to do anything with it?'

'No,' I say. 'I want to teach. I've always wanted to teach.'

'No, you used to tell me you were going to be an artist – an illustrator – but you planned to train as a teacher to have something to fall back on. I've always remembered because that was the first time I'd heard that expression – "something to fall back on", I mean.'

'I don't like that expression,' Bex says. 'It always sounds like having something to do if the thing you really want to do doesn't work out. But I think you should stick at the thing you really want to do until it does work out. Because if you really want to do it, it will work out eventually.'

The waiter arrives with our burgers. The plates are oval and huge and we spend a couple of minutes exclaiming about the amount of food before Oscar and Bex dig in and I say, 'I don't think that's true. I don't think that just because you want to do something you're automatically going to succeed. You might not even be any good at it. You've seen all those people on *The X Factor* saying it's their life's dream to sing and then they open their mouths and sound like cats being murdered.'

'That's true,' Oscar says, 'but I think Bex meant when you *are* actually talented at something.'

'But how do you know you really are?' I say, putting my burger down before I've managed to take a bite. 'Those *X Factor* people think they're talented and it's only when they've been humiliated on TV that they learn they're really not – actually sometimes even then they still don't get it. They keep saying "This is my dream!" like just the fact that it's their dream means that it should come true, no matter what.'

'But you know you can draw,' Bex says. 'Don't you?'

'I used to think I could,' I say.

And then I do take a bite of my burger to stop myself from saying anything else. It's absolutely delicious. Sort of soft and sloppy and much tastier than any burger I've ever had from a fast-food place.

'You used to be really confident about your art,' Oscar says.

Hearing him say 'your art' completely unselfconsciously makes me shudder a bit. I'd forgotten he was like that. Utterly unembarrassed about the things he loves and with no false modesty at all. I can't imagine being like that.

'Was I really?'

He nods, his mouth full of burger. 'You used to show me stuff and say "I'm really proud of this one" and that kind of thing. I liked your confidence. I always thought you'd do well because you wouldn't let anyone put you off. So I'm surprised...'

I shrug. 'I suppose I just got realistic.'

'I don't want to be realistic,' Bex says. 'I'd rather be a dreamer.'

'Well, that's evident,' I tell her, smiling.

'Don't worry,' she says, through a mouthful of burger bun. 'When I'm rich and famous, I'll set you up in your own artist's studio and you can draw and paint all day long.'

I grin. She's sweet, my sister, even if she is in a world of her own. But I'm also a little bit surprised at how the idea of my own studio thrills me. It's so long since I've even thought about art that I'd forgotten how much I used to love it. Maybe I will try drawing again. Just to see if I am good at it. See if I enjoy it.

After we've finished eating, we go next door to Small World Books. It's ages since I've had a good browse around a bookshop and while Bex is engrossed in the Theatre and Film section and Oscar is looking at who-knows-what, I wander around, picking up books that look interesting and flicking through a box of vintage postcards. Near the till, there's a whole shelf of plain notebooks and

I can't resist having a good look. One of the things I used to love about drawing was finding the perfect sketchbook. It had to have the right combination of paper and bendy spine. I used to hate drawing in a book only to find the pen marks had come through to the other side of the paper and my second pet hate was aching hands caused by having to hold open a too-stiff spine.

It is odd how I've pretty much stopped drawing altogether. I don't even really know why I did. I know the art teacher knocked my confidence, but that shouldn't have made me give up. I'm sure if someone told Bex she couldn't act, she'd just be determined to prove them wrong, so why did I let myself give up so easily? I have no idea.

I keep browsing and, around the next bookshelf, find Oscar. He's looking at astronomy books.

'Ah,' I say. 'You're a Libra, I remember. Dreamy, cautious, gorgeous. Or was that gormless?'

'First of all,' he says, without looking round at me. 'I'm a Leo – sexiest sign in the zodiac. Second of all, this is astronomy, not astrology.'

'I know,' I say. 'I'm not a total dunce. What ya

looking at these for?' And then I suddenly remember and start to laugh. 'No. Way.'

'Yes way,' he says, still without turning round, but I can see that the tops of his ears have gone red, so I know he's blushing.

'You still want to be an astronaut?'

'I want to do something in that area, yes. Since you don't know the difference between astronomy and astrology this bit of news may have passed you by, but the US doesn't currently have a space programme.'

'Right,' I say. 'I knew that.' At least I think I did. 'So what does that mean?'

'It means that the job I planned to do – that I've dreamed of doing since I was a kid – is now quite unlikely to be possible. Here, at least. But there's plenty of other stuff I can do and I intend to do it.'

'So how do you...?' I wave my hand vaguely at the bookshelves.

Oscar knows what I mean. 'Work really hard in maths and sciences and then, I don't know, pray, cross my fingers...'

'Wish on a star?'

He grins. 'That sounds like a plan.'

'Excellent.'

'You don't really see so many stars in LA, though – too much light pollution.'

'That's ironic. Stars on the ground, but none in the sky.'

He laughs. 'I'm not going to bother making a wish on Alex Hall, if that's what you mean. And I'm learning Russian – the Russian space programme is still healthy and being able to speak Russian would be a definite advantage.'

'OK,' I say. 'That's really cool. Say something in Russian.'

'*Nyet*,' he says, and I laugh.

'You don't think I'm like someone on *The X Factor*?' he says. 'Kidding themselves?'

'Well, I'm not going to lie to you. The idea of you being a spaceman makes me want to laugh. Quite a lot. But if that's what you want to do, who am I to tell you you can't?'

'Indeed,' he says, smiling. 'Particularly since you know absolutely nothing about it. And it's astronaut, not spaceman.'

'I know,' I say. 'That one was just to wind you up. I think it's cool, honestly.'

Bex appears with an armful of books, including a biography of Alex Hall.

'Seriously?' I say. 'Isn't he about twenty? What's he done?'

'He's nineteen,' she says. 'I think it's mainly photos.'

Fair enough. He's certainly nice to look at. I follow her over to the desk so she can pay.

As we're waiting, I grab one of the notebooks – it has a vintage photo of the Venice Beach sign on the cover – and add it to Bex's pile of books. I might not draw in it, but it's good to know I'll have a perfect book if I ever do get the urge.

As we're walking back along the Boardwalk, Oscar suddenly shouts something incomprehensible and darts off across some grass towards a skatepark. Bex and I just stand and watch him go, until he turns around, gestures at us to follow him and shouts, 'Come on!' We follow him.

The skatepark is pretty cool. It's not like the one

near my old school, which is basically two inverted slabs of concrete; this one is sculptured. All hills and valleys and curves. If people weren't skating on it, it would probably look like a pretty cool piece of public art. (When people aren't skating on the one at home, it looks like a massive example of vandalism.)

'What are we looking at?' I ask Oscar, but then I see. Tabby appears from out of a dip, hovers in mid-air long enough to spot us and then disappears from sight again.

'Was that Tabby?' Bex asks.

Oscar nods. 'She's fantastic. Sam skates here too, but he must be at work if Tab's here.'

Tabby appears again, further away this time, skirting the edge of the furthest curve. She's leaning at about forty-five degrees and moving pretty quickly along the concrete, but it looks completely effortless. The skateboard makes a swishing sound that's almost hypnotic. She swoops out of sight then reappears, before leaping over the top of one of the crests and landing on her feet, with her skateboard in her hand, right in front of us.

'Hi!' she says. To Oscar.

'Wow, that was amazing!' Bex says, grinning.

'Thanks.' Tabby smiles back at her.

'You make it look so easy,' I tell her.

'It is pretty easy,' she says, shrugging. 'Once you've practised for a few years.'

'Wow,' Bex says again. 'I think I'd be too scared.'

'Nah, you just have to wear a lot of padding when you first start. I bashed my ass so much, my mom used to make me pad my pants. But I hardly ever fall any more.'

'Tab's won competitions and been on TV. She's a bit of a skating star,' Oscar says.

Tabby dips her head and gives him a shove as if she's embarrassed, but she looks pleased. Between that and Oscar calling her 'Tab', I wonder if there's something going on between them. They definitely look good together – her with her black hair and red lips and him with his red hair. I feel a bit strange about it. I'm not jealous, obviously, but I have that feeling you sometimes get when you introduce two friends who didn't previously know each other and you don't want them to go off without you. Which is ridiculous, since I haven't even seen Oscar for years and if anyone should be feeling like that, it's Tabby.

I'm distracted from my thoughts when a boy who looks about Bex's age trips backwards off his skateboard, which flies up in the air and hits the railings we're leaning against, sending a vibration through my hands. When he comes to collect it, he looks almost tearful.

'And you have to make sure you know what you're doing before you try it on the park,' Tabby says to us. The boy looks a bit shamefaced as he leaves.

'You should definitely try it though,' Tabby tells Bex. 'Even if it's just on the bike path or somewhere. When you really get good at it it feels like flying.'

Bex nods. I can see from her face that she's planning to buy a skateboard as soon as possible. She is so keen to throw herself into LA life. She's so unlike me.

Chapter Ten

We've only been home a few minutes when a courier brings a parcel for Bex from Emily.

There's a note telling us that Wednesday would be good for going to the studio and giving us Jordan's numbers, and there's a DVD of *Stellar Highway*, Alex's show.

A few minutes later, Mum gets back and she's brought takeaway Vietnamese food, so we dish it all out on the coffee table and put the DVD in the player. We're just about to watch it when Bex's phone rings. It's Dad and she starts telling him about the meeting with Emily. I pick at the fried tofu slices Mum loves.

'She was wonderful today, wasn't she?' Mum says, picking a bit of everything for her plate.

'Bex? Yeah. She's so confident, it's amazing.'

Mum nods, her mouth full, and then says, 'That's the main thing your dad and I wanted for you two. We just wanted you to have the confidence to do whatever you wanted in life.'

Bex frowns at us for talking while she's on the phone and walks through to the kitchen.

I fold another tofu slice into my mouth and ask Mum, 'Do you know why I stopped drawing?'

Her eyes go wide. 'Oh! No. What made you think of that?'

'Oscar and Bex were talking about it today. They think I gave up too easily. Bex said that Dad said so.'

'Ah,' Mum says. She puts her plate back on the table and looks at me. 'I always thought your dad was a bit hard on you about it.'

'Really?' I don't remember that.

She nods. 'Your dad doesn't really do anything by half measures, you know? And I know he thought you were extremely talented – we both did. I think he thought you should be taking it more seriously than you were.'

I frown. 'I don't really remember him pressuring me about it.'

'No? I don't remember specific examples, but I do remember you being upset once or twice because you'd been proud of something and he'd pointed out the faults.'

And I do remember that. But Dad was always like that. If I got ninety per cent on a test, he'd ask what happened to the other ten per cent. It was annoying, but I thought I was used to it. Is that what happened? Is that what made me stop?

'He was disappointed when you didn't go ahead with the art class, I know that,' Mum says.

I slide one of the plastic dishes over to my end of the coffee table.

'He'd hate to think you stopped because of him,' Mum says.

I look at her. I don't know that I did, but it's certainly possible.

'Have you spoken to him since we got here?' she asks.

I shake my head.

'You could go and have a word now?'

I can hear Bex saying goodbye, telling Dad she loves him.

'No, that's OK,' I say. 'The food's getting cold.'

The titles of *Stellar Highway* show Alex riding a motorbike along a coast road that's wreathed in fog.

'Oh, dear,' I say. 'Maybe we shouldn't watch this. I might not be able to look him in the face at the studios.'

'Give it a chance, for goodness' sake,' Mum says, smiling at me.

Bex is ignoring me and staring transfixed at the screen, no doubt picturing herself appearing in this very show in the near future.

The titles end and the show starts with Alex lying in bed. His long eyelashes are fluttering and he starts tossing his head from side to side. And then there's one of those flash close-up things right to his face so you feel like you're going inside his head. There's a close-up on his eyes, which are a really unusual colour. I didn't notice in Emily's office, but they almost look bronze. Then suddenly the scene changes to a bright square in what looks like Mexico – multi-coloured houses, railings around a small park with flowers woven through the bars. And Alex standing in front of an enormous tree, looking puzzled.

'What's the deal?' I say. 'Is this a dream?'

Bex shushes me aggressively and I look at Mum and grin.

The show does actually turn out to be pretty entertaining. Alex's character – his name is Luke – is a journalism student and star of the college paper who, whenever he falls asleep, astrally travels elsewhere, generally to the scene of a crime, if the flashbacks are anything to go by.

In Mexico, he hangs out with a group of American teens there on spring break. One of them dies of an overdose and Luke knows that the drug was given to them by one of the other teens, who then claims the dead kid bought it from a Mexican bigwig. Luke has the story for his paper and also has to work out an explanation for how he got it. That bit's not entirely convincing, but the rest of it's pretty good. It's easy to see how Alex became so popular so quickly. He's charming, funny and sexy – and he takes his shirt off a lot.

I'm looking forward to the studio visit even more now.

Chapter Eleven

I'm woken in the morning by my mobile vibrating off my bedside table and onto the floor. I grope for it, screwing my eyes up against the bright sunshine that's pouring in through the gap in the curtains. It's not right, sunshine first thing in the morning – it's against the natural order of things.

I find my phone and make out that it's Oscar calling, before I press the green button.

'Did you forget?' he says.

'Whaa?'

'Grand tour? Today? We were meant to go yesterday, but we set Bex on her path to fame and fortune instead?'

'What time is it?' I groan, swinging my legs off the side of the bed.

'Ten,' he says. 'Tour starts at eleven and we've got to get to Santa Monica yet.'

'Where are you?' I head for the bathroom and wince when I see my reflection. My hair's standing on end and yesterday's mascara is smeared under each eye.

'I'm outside,' he says. 'On your dock.'

'Seriously?'

'Yep. Do you want to take a rain check, as they say round here?'

'No, no,' I say. 'Thanks. I'll let you in. Hang on a minute.'

I end the call and go through to Bex's room. She's sitting cross-legged on her pillow with her laptop balanced on a pile of books at the end of the bed. As soon as she sees me, she holds up one finger behind her back to tell me not to speak. She's obviously recording.

I roll my eyes and head downstairs to let Oscar in, trying to smooth my hair down with my hands on the way. In the living room, I pull back one of the curtains and am again blinded by the bright sunshine. A picture of home pops into my head. The front door of our old house. Rain on the red tiles of the front path. It seems like a different world.

I slide open the door and Oscar comes through. He's wearing long blue shorts and a red T-shirt with the Starbucks logo, only it says STAR WARS and has a picture of a Stormtrooper instead of the mermaid.

'Thank god,' he says. 'Your neighbours were starting to look at me funny.'

'They probably thought you were an enormous garden gnome,' I say.

He does finger guns at me and says, 'I'm not sure I'm willing to be insulted by a woman who's not wearing any trousers.' But then he looks down at my legs and blushes.

'I'll go and get dressed then,' I tell him. 'And I'll send Bex down. She's filming herself on her laptop.'

'Oh hey!' Oscar says, as I'm halfway through the kitchen. 'Pride of place!'

I'd put the photo from the big wheel on the

mantelpiece. Since our stuff's all in storage, it's the only photo we have.

'You do appreciate me,' Oscar says, and pretends to cry.

I shake my head – he's such a dork – and run up the stairs to get dressed.

The tour bus is small, only about twelve seats. I sit with Bex and Oscar sits behind us. An Australian girl who looks to be in her early twenties and a German couple get on and sit on the other side of the bus. We wait there for about twenty minutes while the driver chats on his phone, presumably waiting for more people to turn up. He's got a strong Latin American accent and a really infectious giggle. I don't know who he's talking to, but apparently they're hilarious. Eventually he stops chatting, gives up waiting and we set off.

He drives us past the canals, which feels quite weird. I keep wanting to tell the other people on the bus, 'We live here!' We see a big scary-ass clown ballerina statue that was apparently in the Sandra Bullock film *Speed* and then the driver drops us back at Venice Beach for twenty minutes.

'Ah,' Oscar says. 'I didn't realise it did this. We could've started here.'

Since we live here, we don't bother walking down to the Boardwalk like the others, we get a coffee instead. We sit outside people-watching and I text Jessie a photo of someone skateboarding while hanging on to the back of a car. We'd wanted to see someone doing that in New York, but never did.

When the others come back to the bus, they're horrified by the Boardwalk. The German couple declare it 'disgusting' and the Australian isn't much more complimentary.

Oscar grins at me and whispers, 'It'll be the weed that horrified them.'

'They should've stayed a bit longer,' I say, 'and breathed a bit deeper.'

We drive along the Pacific Coast Highway back to Santa Monica and then up towards the Hollywood Hills to see some celebrity homes. The guide talks all the time and slows down outside huge, impressive houses, but most of the time all we can see is the gate and a bit of the roof. It's interesting, though, just seeing how the other half lives. The houses are much closer together than I would have expected. I don't suppose Leonardo DiCaprio waves to JLo as he picks up his paper at the gate, but he probably could if he wanted to.

Opposite one house there's a crowd of paparazzi, some of them leaning against a wall and some sitting on the ground, looking bored.

'Whose house is that?' the Australian woman asks the driver.

'Oh, that's a new star,' he says. 'Young and very famous.'

We all wait for him to tell us the star's name, but I'm not sure he really knows. 'Like Robert Pattinson from the *Twilight* films?' he says.

'Robert Pattinson?!' Bex shrieks. She had a poster of him on her wall in the old house.

'No,' the driver says. 'Like him, but not him. He's in a TV show and he rides a motorbike in space—'

'*Alex Hall?*' the Australian girl yells, almost leaping out of her seat. 'I love him!'

'Yes! That's him!' the driver says, looking back over his shoulder and grinning.

I swivel round in my seat to try to get a good look at Alex Hall's house, but I can only see the roof and a bit of an arched window. Not bad, though, considering he's not that much older than me. I wonder what he's really like. He seemed nice enough in Emily's office, but we should get a better idea when we go to the studio. I just hope he's nice to Bex.

A couple of minutes later, the driver announces that we're passing UCLA.

'Is that where Mum is?' Bex asks us.

Oscar nods.

Bex and I both crane our heads to look out over the campus. All I can see is trees and some terracotta-coloured buildings. The driver is talking about how many students attend and the size of the campus. It's big, basically.

'Have you been there?' Bex asks Oscar.

He nods. 'It's pretty cool. We should definitely get them to take us up there one day, have a look around. They have some events on sometimes too. You know, presentations and stuff.'

Bex is still looking over at the university when the driver starts yelling that there's a celebrity in the car next to us. We try to peer through the darkened windows, but can't tell who it is.

'Is it Taylor Lautner?' Bex says.

'Yes!' the driver yells. 'From *Twilight*!'

'I don't think it is,' Oscar says, and I'm not sure it is either, but the driver and Bex seem pretty convinced so we don't argue.

The next stop is Grauman's Theatre and the Hollywood Walk of Fame. Bex is beside herself, getting us to take photos of her posing with her hands in the imprints of various stars. She gets a bit tearful at the Marilyn Monroe plaque and then just stares in awe at the Meryl Streep one. Bex adores Meryl Streep, mainly since *Mamma Mia*, but she's watched a lot of her older movies on DVD and once said she'd love a career like hers. She's ambitious, my sister, I'll say that for her.

Oscar makes us laugh by putting his hand inside Arnold Schwarzenegger's gigantic prints – Oscar's hands are about half the size, as are his feet. My hands are the same size as Emma Watson's. Oscar takes a photo of me posing next to Cary Grant's plaque and I text it to Jessie. She and her mum love an old film of his called *An Affair to Remember*, which is about Cary Grant's character arranging to meet a woman at the top of the Empire State Building, but she doesn't turn up because she gets hit by a taxi. It's supposed to be romantic, apparently.

Bex tells me she's sending her Meryl Streep photo to Dad and I scroll through my phone and find his number. Even when Jessie and her mum weren't getting on, they always watched old films together, so they had that to talk about. I wish I could text Dad something casual as if he never left, as if everything was fine, but I just can't. Not yet. I lock the keyboard and put my phone back in my pocket.

We walk down Hollywood Boulevard, looking at the stars on the pavement. I knew about the Walk of Fame, but I'm surprised at just how many stars there are; there's one every other step. Bex hops from one to another like the opposite of not stepping on the pavement cracks. When we ask her what she's doing, she says it's good luck. I don't know if she's read that or just made it up. The stars are pretty cool, I must admit, but it's kind of weird to see people just walking down the pavement as if there's nothing unusual. Is it really such a great honour to have your name on the ground for people to walk over? I'm not so sure.

All along the road, people are dressed up as various characters and posing for photos for money. They're all rubbish though. There's a tiny guy dressed as Spider-Man, but his costume's badly fitted and frayed. I've seen better Spider-Men at kids' parties. There's a woman who I know, by the green dress and the toy frog, is supposed to be the princess from *The Princess and the Frog*, but she's about twenty years too old and she looks really pissed off. We dodge a rather chubby Captain Jack Sparrow and an equally unconvincing Marilyn Monroe and nip into the Kodak Center to get away from the pavement crowds.

'What's this place?' Bex says, turning in a circle and looking up at the ceiling lights.

'It's just a shopping centre with a cinema,' Oscar says, 'but it's pretty cool. I thought we could get a coffee or something.'

We follow Oscar through to an open courtyard which has multi-coloured fountains in the centre, plaster elephants on plinths, twinkly lights everywhere and a massive *X Factor* billboard featuring Simon Cowell.

'One day that'll be me,' Bex says, staring up at the billboard.

'What? Too-white teeth and trousers up to your chin?' I ask.

She flaps her hand at me. 'No. My name in lights.'

Cowell's name's not actually in lights – it's just a billboard – but I don't bother to correct her. Who knows, she could be right.

Chapter Twelve

Jordan, Alex's PA, meets us at the studio gate and gives us visitor passes.

Bex is so overexcited I think she's lost the power of speech, but her facial expression could be described as 'ecstatic' and has been that way since she spotted the Warner Brothers water tower from a couple of wide leafy streets away.

'I'm just going to walk you over to the soundstage,' Jordan tells us. He's tall and skinny with small, round-rimmed glasses and a very preppy outfit – chinos and a white shirt. 'Alex is filming right now, but I'm going to show you around a bit and then we can get lunch. After that, if you're interested, I thought you might like to take the studio tour. Does that sound OK?'

'That sounds wonderful,' I say.

We start walking and it seems utterly surreal to be here. The huge, square, windowless buildings seem incredibly familiar and there actually are people zipping around in little golf carts. It is absolutely and utterly what I imagined a movie studio would look like.

Bex grabs my arm and points at the corner of the beige building on our left. Next to the door, there's a plaque: THE FRIENDS STAGE.

'Ah, you're *Friends* fans?' Jordan asks. 'Yes, they filmed there for eight out of the ten seasons. For the first two, they were still using that soundstage for *The Facts of Life*. You know that show?'

We both shake our heads and Jordan grins. 'Yeah, it was before my time too. But George Clooney was in it!'

I look back at the steps leading up to the door to the studio and imagine Courteney Cox, Jennifer Aniston and the rest walking up there on their way to make my all-time favourite TV show and I can't believe we're really here.

We walk diagonally to another beige building and

then in through a huge roller door, like a garage door.

'Hey!' Jordan shouts to a woman further down the building. 'You know this door's open?'

She nods and shouts something that I don't catch, but Jordan's not impressed. 'These doors are always meant to be kept closed,' he mumbles. Once we're inside it reminds me of backstage at theatre shows Bex has done in the past. The plain wooden backs of scenery and the same smell – of dust and make-up and lights. Bex squeezes my hand. My stomach is flipping with excitement so I can't imagine how she must be feeling.

Jordan turns and puts his finger to his lips and we follow him down the passageway and then out into an enormous room, one side of which is a set that I recognise as Alex's – or rather Luke's – bedroom in *Stellar Highway*.

'Ah, it's OK,' Jordan says. 'They're on a break.'

I look up at the lights and metal tracks running around the roof. This place is huge.

Jordan shows us over to where Alex is sitting, fiddling with his phone. He looks up and grins and I feel my legs wobble. 'Hey, you made it!'

'Thanks so much for letting us do this,' I say.

He smiles. 'No problem. Was the ride in OK?'

'Great, thanks,' I say. A man named Jem picked us up in a smart black car with tinted windows and one of those glass dividers between the front and back. Like a taxi, but fabulous.

'You OK, Bex?' Alex asks my sister.

I look at Bex. Her mouth is open, but she still hasn't managed to speak.

'I think she's a bit overwhelmed,' I tell Alex.

'I was like that the first time I came here,' he tells her. 'I was shaking so much the camera picked it up. And Jordan here had to keep me supplied with lemon slices to stop my lips from sticking to my teeth.'

'I've done that!' Bex says. Probably because it's so long since she last spoke, it comes out pretty loud and we all laugh. 'In panto,' she adds, more quietly.

'You've done panto?' Alex says, grinning. 'I've read about that. It sounds crazy.'

'It was pretty great,' Bex says, smiling.

'So Jordan's told you about the tour?' Alex asks.

'Yes. It sounds fantastic,' I tell him. 'Thank you so much.'

'No worries. Jordan's the man – he'll look after you.'

He touches me on the arm and I get that tingling feeling again. It's so strong that I want to look down and see if his fingers have left a mark, but I contain myself.

Someone yells for Alex.

'Back to work,' he says, still smiling.

Jordan offers me Alex's seat and I sit. It's still warm. Bex and Jordan sit down too and, for the next hour, we watch Alex filming.

When we watched the show at home, I would have said the character was pretty similar to Alex. Watching him now, I see him change when the cameras are on. I start to see a difference between Alex and Luke. Luke seems older, more intense, even his body language is different. It's so interesting. And a little bit weird. It must be hard to get used to flipping between personalities like that. The scene they're filming is between Alex – I mean, Luke – and his roommate. The character's called Jason, I'm not sure about the actor.

Jason is trying to get Luke to tell him how he

keeps getting such fantastic scoops and obviously Luke is struggling to work out what to tell him. Jason's also on the paper and if Luke has got some sort of fantastically reliable contact, Jason wants to know why he won't share it with him.

The guy playing Jason would probably be considered incredibly good-looking if he was in his own show – he's tall and kind of lanky with cropped hair and really sharp cheekbones – but next to Alex he only looks OK. I can see, looking at Alex, what people mean when they talk about presence and charisma. You can't not look at him.

And after staring at him pretty constantly for about an hour, it's pretty weird when they wrap the scene and he walks over to us, says, 'Lunch?' and claps Jordan on the shoulder.

It's almost like seeing someone walk out of the TV screen (which I always thought would be really cool).

We follow Alex through to another room within the same building, where a huge table is set out with all sorts of different food on it. It's like a buffet at the best wedding ever. There's smoked salmon, pasta, pizza, various salads, baked potatoes, doughnuts, chocolate, pretzels, sushi, plates and plates of sandwiches – basically everything you could possibly want to eat for lunch.

We follow Alex and grab some food. There's actually so much choice that I find it really hard to decide.

'The sushi's really good,' Alex says, turning to smile at me.

I grab a dish of sushi and a bottle of mineral water. Bex has got mainly salad with some nachos and a can of Coke.

'I usually eat in my trailer,' Alex tells us. 'Is that OK with you guys?'

'I'm coming too,' Jordan says, grinning. 'No scandal.'

We follow Alex to his trailer, which is almost exactly like the trailers you see in films – white on the outside with a couple of little steps and like a flash caravan on the inside with shiny wood and white surfaces.

'You're so tidy!' Bex says, as Jordan gestures for us to sit down at the table.

Alex laughs. 'Not what my mom says. I think someone tidies for me while I'm working.'

'Usually me,' Jordan says, smiling.

We sit in silence for a couple of minutes while we're all eating.

'Do you get food like this every day?' I ask.

Alex nods. 'On my first job, I couldn't believe there was so much food. I ate so much that I was falling asleep when we were filming. The director was pi—' He stops himself and grins. 'Well, he wasn't happy.'

'It happens a lot though,' Jordan says, dipping his head as if someone from the gossip mags might be listening. 'There are a lot of A-list stars who can't resist the catering. I think it's because they remember when they were young and hungry.'

Alex laughs. 'If the food's there you're gonna eat it, right? How's the sushi?' he asks me.

'Really good. I don't think I've ever had real sushi before. Only the stuff from the supermarkets.'

'No?' Alex says. 'You've never been to a sushi bar?'

I shake my head. 'Terrible, isn't it? At my age.'

He grins and I feel a little twinge in my stomach – he really has got a fantastic smile.

'You have to go soon,' he says. 'Where are you living?'

I tell him Venice and his face lights up. 'There's a great sushi place in Venice. On Windward Circle? You have to go.'

'All right,' I say. 'I'll add it to my bucket list.'

He grins at me and then asks Bex if Emily's sent her out on anything yet. She manages to get over her nerves and tell him that she hasn't. Then she talks a bit about the stuff she's done in the past and what she hopes to do in the future. She's got big plans. She basically wants to be the new Miley Cyrus, with acting, music and commercial deals.

When she's finished, Alex asks me, 'Have you got big plans too?'

I pull a face. 'No. Not really. I've always wanted to be a teacher. Well, actually, I thought that's what I wanted, but then my friend Oscar reminded me that I wanted to be an artist – an illustrator – but I stopped drawing a while ago. So, basically, I don't know.'

'Is Oscar your boyfriend?' Alex asks, which is very much not the bit of my rambling that I expected him to pick up on.

'Oh no,' I say. 'He was my best friend growing up and now our mum works with his dad, so he's pretty much my only friend in LA.'

Alex nods and the way he's looking at me makes my stomach go a bit fluttery. He really is stupidly good-looking. Nice, too. He didn't need to take time out of his day to hang out with us, but he did.

When we've all finished eating, Alex and Jordan take us on a little tour of the soundstage, pointing out the curtain that acts as the view from his character's bedroom – it even has thinner bits of fabric where the windows are so that if it's supposed to be night, they can shine light through it – and to the set of the gardens behind Luke's apartment building, which I saw on the show and never would have guessed were filmed indoors. There are lights to represent the moon and the sun on tracks so they can move them depending on their position in the sky. Oscar would love that. It's all so interesting and a little bit scary – I don't think I'll ever believe anything I see on TV again.

We hear someone yelling for Alex. He rolls his eyes.

'So I'd better get back to work,' he says.

'Thanks so much,' I tell him. 'You've been really lovely.'

He stares at me for a second and then says, 'I love your accent.'

'Thanks,' I say, and I actually feel my eyebrows shoot up. 'I like yours too.'

He puts his hand on my shoulder, says, 'See you later. Enjoy it.' And he's gone.

'How long have you been working with Alex?' Bex asks Jordan as we start walking.

My legs are moving too, but my head is all over the place. Was Alex just flirting? If it had been any other boy, I would have thought the hand on the shoulder was a definite sign, but I don't know. He couldn't be flirting with me, surely. Not when he could have any girl he wanted.

Jordan and Bex chat away as Jordan walks us out to the main building, where I take a photo of Bex with the huge bronze statues of Bugs Bunny and Daffy Duck. Jordan takes us inside the building and introduces us to our guide for the tour. They're all so professional and friendly and everything seems to run so smoothly here. It's like a completely different world. I wonder if it's like this all the time or if we're getting special treatment because of Alex.

The guide – a woman named Jenna – takes us out onto one of the little open buses we've already noticed buzzing around the studio, where the rest of the tour group are gathered. There are ten of us altogether and I think the others are all American. We drive back through the studios. Jenna tells us that the car park we were dropped off in was used as the helicopter landing pad in *ER* and shows us the *Friends* building, but this time she stops so we can get our photos taken with the sign. I get Bex to take one of me and I text it to Jessie. Then we go to see an exhibition of cars used in films – they have the Union Jack car from one of the Austin Powers films – and they demonstrate how green screen works by taking a photo of us in front of one and then adding the Hogwarts Express behind us. It's like the photo we had taken on the pier, but much more realistic. I wish Oscar was here – he'd love it so much he'd probably get it put on a T-shirt.

From there we go to the prop building and Jenna tells us about all the props they have there and how they're used. It's so interesting, particularly since I'd never really thought about that level of attention to detail. In Alex's character's apartment, for instance, every single thing has been chosen by a set designer: the sheets, the bed, the carpet, the pictures on the walls, the cutlery he uses to eat his food. Everything. And it's all chosen to reflect the character's personality.

And then Jenna takes us into Central Perk from *Friends* and it's really weird because it doesn't look like Central Perk at all. It looks like maybe someone tried to recreate the set from memory, but it's all just a bit off. I take a couple of photos anyway and one of Bex next to the sign and then Jenna drives us around the studio a bit more. Alex's show is filming outside now – it's meant to be a New York street, but Jenna says the same street has been used to represent all manner of different places. Bex can't keep still, she's so excited.

'This could be you soon,' I tell her.

'Can you imagine it?' she says, beaming. 'Even just being here is like a dream, I don't know what it would be like to actually be involved in a show.'

At the end of the tour, we're shown into the museum, which features mainly costumes from film and TV downstairs and Harry Potter stuff upstairs. Bex runs off up the stairs and I wander around the costumes. I can totally see what attracts Bex to all this. There are costumes worn by Bette Davis, by George Clooney and by Ellen Page in *Juno*. I like the history of it all. And the glamour, of course. But pretending for a living seems a little bit odd to me in a way I don't think it does to Bex. Maybe I just think that because I can't do it.

I'm looking at clothes worn by Blake Lively in *Gossip Girl* when Jordan finds me.

'Hey,' he says. 'Did you enjoy the tour? Where's your sister?'

We find Bex staring glassy-eyed at an original Harry Potter Sorting Hat and coax her back downstairs and out of the museum.

'Alex has just got a couple more scenes to do, so we'll go and hang out and then Jem will take you back. Unless there is anything else you want to see here?'

'I don't think so,' I tell him. 'It's all been brilliant.'

'Maybe... Could we just go back to the shop?' Bex asks. 'I'd like a T-shirt or something, if that's OK.'

'Oh, no problem,' Jordan says. We walk back over there – as we go through the security gate, Bex clutches my arm again. I'm starting to understand this means 'I can't believe this is happening' and it does feel pretty cool. Particularly when some people on the way in smile and say hello to us as if we totally belong there.

I buy a Harry Potter T-shirt that says EXPELLIARMUS on it for Oscar and then, while Bex is running around the shop trying to choose something, I scroll through the photos on my phone. Even though when we were there, Central Perk looked absolutely nothing like it does on TV, it looks exactly right on my phone. If I hadn't seen it with my own eyes, I wouldn't have believed it. I show Jordan and he laughs. 'Yep, that's the magic of TV. They say the camera never lies, but when you start working in this industry you learn real quick that things aren't always what they seem.'

Once Bex has finished shopping, we walk back to the soundstage. Alex is filming another outdoor scene. He's repairing his motorbike and, yes, he's got his shirt off. I saw him shirtless when I watched the show, but that was entirely different. I was watching it with my mum, for one, and also it was on the TV – he wasn't *right in front of me*. Now I feel myself blush and my palms are sweating. I really hope he puts his shirt back on before he comes over to talk to us. (And at the same time I hope he doesn't.) I even have a brief thought of quickly snapping a photo on my phone, even though we're under strict instructions to keep our phones off on the soundstage. I'd quite like to have a permanent reminder of this moment. I'll just have to stare really hard and try to imprint it on my memory. Instead an image of a few of the boys from home pops into my mind. Alex makes them look like a different species.

When the scene's over, Jordan takes Bex to introduce her to the director and Alex comes over to me. He's put a shirt on, which is probably for the best.

'That was really good,' I say. I'm quite surprised my voice comes out at the right pitch.

Alex smiles. 'Thanks. This show's kind of obsessed with showing me shirtless. It's pretty embarrassing.'

He doesn't look embarrassed, he looks quite

pleased with himself, but I'm not surprised.

'Yeah,' I say. 'I've seen that jeans ad. I know you're probably actually really shy.'

He laughs. 'Hey, that ad was art.'

'Oh, I know,' I say, smiling. 'I've seen that kind of art before. But usually it features women and it's on the top shelf in the newsagent's.'

Alex shrugs and grins. 'It pays the bills.'

'Hey, I'm not judging,' I say. 'Well, maybe a bit.'

We grin at each other for a couple of seconds and the feeling of anticipation in my stomach is almost painful.

'So, I'm going to grab a shower,' Alex says.

I take a step backwards. Right. He wasn't flirting. Of course he wasn't. But now I'm picturing him in the shower, which really isn't helpful.

'Do you think I could get your number?' Alex says.

I feel my breath catch. 'What?'

'Your number? I was thinking maybe we could go out for sushi sometime.'

'Right.' I nod and remind myself to breathe. 'I don't think that will be a problem,' I say.

Chapter Thirteen

Oscar's house isn't on the canals – it's on one of the wide tree-lined streets we passed when we arrived. He's been doing some extra shifts at work, so I haven't seen him since Tuesday.

He opens the door. He's wearing a University of Gallifrey T-shirt and camouflage trousers.

'Whoa!' I say. 'Where are your legs? Are they... invisible?'

He looks down at himself, starts to say 'What?' and then realises. 'You're very funny,' he says. 'You should try an open-mic night. You probably wouldn't get bottled off.'

I grin and follow him inside. The hall is bright and

clean and I find that I'm quite surprised. I don't know why, but I was expecting it to be dark and messy. Maybe because I'm not used to the idea of Michael and Oscar living on their own. Oscar's mum was always super house-proud and I think I expected them to be rebelling.

'No Bex?' he says.

'No. She and Mum have gone along to an open casting with Emily. She's not auditioning, Emily just wanted her to see how it all works.'

'Cool,' Oscar says. 'Is that usual?'

'No idea. Mum seems to think all the preparation's good though, so who knows.'

'Has she recovered from Wednesday yet?' he asks.

'Just about,' I think. 'At least she's stopped beginning every sentence with "When we were at the studio..."'

He laughs. 'Well, she did see an original Sorting Hat. That's not something you just get over.'

'Which reminds me,' I say. 'When we were at the studio...I got you a present.'

I hand him the Warner Brothers bag. He takes

the T-shirt out, shakes it out so he can see the front and says, 'I love it! Thanks!'

'I tried to nick the Sorting Hat, but the security was too tight.' I smile.

He holds the T-shirt up to himself and says, 'Is it me?'

'You just need the little round glasses,' I say.

I follow him down the hall.

'So this is where the magic happens,' he says, glancing at me over his shoulder.

'What?' I say. 'The whole house? Kinky!'

He looks back at me again, with one eyebrow raised, but ruins it by blushing.

We go through to the living room, which actually does remind me of the house he and Michael lived in back in Bramhall. Some of the same pictures are on the wall – including a photo of me and Oscar when we were about three. We're sitting on the floor with our legs out straight in front of us. We've both got dirty bare feet and we're grinning into the camera like chimps.

The kitchen's small and clean and painted bright yellow. Oscar passes me a Coke out of the fridge

– a bottled Coke; he takes the lid off with a bottle opener mounted on the wall – and then opens French doors to the garden. It's lovely. Enclosed and leafy, with raised decking and a chimney thing like we have on our terrace. We sit at a little round table on chairs covered with red-and-white-striped fabric.

'Thanks for the T-shirt,' he says again. 'It's great.'

'I thought you'd like it,' I tell him. 'It's good to know you haven't changed completely.'

'What? This is clean on,' he jokes, feebly. 'What do you mean? You think I've changed?'

I laugh. 'Definitely! You're loads more confident. You used to be really self-conscious, but now you're chatting away to Mum, driving in LA, ordering in cafés...'

He wrinkles his nose. 'I don't know. I think I just grew up a bit, maybe. Stopped worrying about what everyone thought about me. Working at the Wok definitely made me more confident, and busking...'

'Busking? You...busk?'

He's blushing again. 'I didn't mean to mention that, it just slipped out. Yeah. I do a bit. That's my other job.'

'What do you do? You sing?'

'Yeah. Just stupid stuff I've made up, mostly. And I play the ukulele.'

'Show me!' I say, bouncing up and down in my seat.

'Hells no!'

'Oscar! Show me!'

He shakes his head. 'You'll see me one of these days – I do it on the Boardwalk – but I'm not doing it now.'

'Why not?' I ask.

'Too shy,' he says, in a tiny voice, looking up at me from under his red fringe.

'Yeah, right.'

'And I'll say no more about that,' he says. He mime-zips his lips, locks them and pretends to throw away the key.

Grinning – he's such a dork – I look around the garden. There are orange and lemon trees and I'm about to ask Oscar if you can eat the oranges when I see him 'unlock' and 'unzip' his mouth, before swigging his Coke.

'Did you just unlock your mouth?' I ask him.

He blushes again and then nods.

'Ha! That's fantastic! I've never seen anyone do that before.'

'Well, you weren't meant to see,' he says.

I laugh. 'I'm sorry to have intruded on a private and not at all mental moment.'

We sit in silence for a couple of minutes and then I blurt out, 'So what's going on with you and Tabby?'

His eyebrows shoot up. 'Nothing! What do you mean?'

'Oh, come on,' I say, laughing. 'You flirt like mad!'

He shakes his head. 'We just mess about.'

'She fancies you.'

He frowns. 'Do you think so?'

'I know so. It's really obvious. You really didn't know?'

'I don't think she does. She's just like that. You know, ruffling my hair and stuff. Sam does it too – do you think he fancies me as well?'

'Maybe. I haven't seen enough of him to know. But Tabby definitely does. I don't think she thinks much of me either.'

'What? Why?'

I shrug. 'Call it female intuition. I think she thinks I've swooped in and she's got her nose pushed out.'

'I think you've got an overactive imagination.'

I shake my head. 'We'll see. But I think she's warm for your form.'

He laughs. 'Oh, god. Never say that again. About anyone. Ever.'

I grin at him.

He swigs the rest of his Coke and says, 'Do you want to go out? The beach?'

'I don't know. How about a house tour?'

'You just want to see my bedroom,' he says, raising one eyebrow.

'You're right. I've been dying to get you up there since I saw you were invisible from the waist down.'

Oscar's bedroom in his old house was so tiny that he made a sign for the door with a picture of Harry Potter's owl and the words THE CUPBOARD UNDER THE STAIRS. It was mainly built-in storage – which his bed fitted into – and hardly any floor space at all. It was kind of cool. I coveted it when I first started hanging out there because everything had a place – there was a cupboard that folded down to make a desk for him to do his homework on, and he had everything he needed within reach of the bed and a TV mounted on the wall, like in a hotel.

His room here is about ten times the size. One wall is covered with posters and cuttings of the planets, the moon and constellations. In his old room he had those glow-in-the-dark stars on his ceiling and that was it.

'So you're really serious about this astronaut thing, then?' I say.

He nods. 'It's my life's ambition to see the earth from space.'

'Do you want to walk on the moon?' He's got a framed poster of the moon in its different phases.

'Well, maybe, yeah. But that's not what I think about. I just think about looking out of that porthole and seeing the earth. All swirling blue and green. Like a marble. It must be incredible.'

'I've just never heard of anyone really wanting to be an astronaut before. It's like when little girls say they want to be a ballerina...'

He nods. 'I know. But it is a real job. Real people

do it. Why shouldn't I be one of them?'

'What's that?' I ask, pointing at a spaceship-like thing that appears on the wall quite a few times.

'That's the International Space Station,' he says.

'Is that...real?' I ask. I was originally going to ask if it was from *Star Trek*, but I could picture the withering look he'd give me (whether it was or not) so I changed my mind.

'Yes, it's real,' he says. 'It's amazing. The first time I saw it going over, it completely blew my mind.'

'How do you see it?'

'You can see it crossing the sky on a clear night. It looks like a star moving really slowly. People are always reporting it as a UFO.'

'Are you sure? You think I've forgotten the time you said you saw Father Christmas's sleigh and the reindeer?'

'I did!' he says, laughing.

'I was so jealous. I can't believe you made it up.'

'You just didn't believe enough,' he says, grinning. 'But honestly, the ISS is possibly even more exciting than flying reindeer. Your mum hasn't told you about it?'

'She might've done,' I say. 'I don't always listen when she talks about work.'

Oscar rolls his eyes. 'But it's fascinating. I don't understand why you wouldn't be interested, particularly when it's so important to your parents.'

I cross over to his window and look down into the garden. 'I don't know. I know it's stupid, but I always saw it as the stuff that kept them away from us. Not just when they were physically away at work, but even when they were home they'd talk about it all the time.' I turn round. 'I know you understand it, but most normal people don't. It's really hard!'

Oscar smiles. 'Some of it is, if you're interested, yes, but so much of it is amazing. Mind-boggling. And you know you don't have to reject it just because your parents love it.'

'I know,' I say. 'And I know I should've grown out of it by now...'

'You remember when you told me the only reason I was interested in space was to impress my dad?'

I wince. 'God, did I? What a bitch.'

Oscar laughs. 'No, you were right, I think. That's probably why I got interested, but it's not why I stayed interested. I just find the whole thing fascinating. And inspiring.'

As he tells me how the pieces of the space station were so enormous that they each had to be sent up to space separately and then assembled up there – which, you know, I'm sure is true if Oscar says it is, but it sounds completely insane to me – I look at the rest of his room. He's got a double bed in the corner with a blue duvet and pillows and a crocheted red blanket that I recognise from his old house. His nan made it when he was a baby and he's always slept with it. On his bedside table is an iPod dock – one of those cube ones with a digital clock – and two framed photos: one of his mum, and one of him and his dad wearing those plastic macs you get free at festivals when it rains.

His bookcase is crammed with books by Neil Gaiman and Terry Pratchett, along with lots and lots of books about space and science.

I spot something on one of the higher shelves and say, 'Hey? Did I do that?'

Oscar comes over to stand next to me. 'The moon?' He reaches up, takes the picture down and hands it to me. 'Yes. Don't you remember?'

'I didn't, but I do now.' It's a pencil drawing and it's actually really good. It's only small, but the detail and shading are excellent.

'You did it inside the card you sent when my mum and dad split up,' he says.

'I can't believe you've got it in a frame,' I say, smiling at him.

'Why not?' he says. 'I love it.'

I stare at the picture for a second and then say, 'I asked Mum if she knew why I'd stopped drawing.'

'Oh yeah?'

I nod. 'She said she thought it was maybe because Dad put too much pressure on me.'

'And what do you think?'

'I think...' I'm embarrassed to find that I'm starting to choke up. 'I think maybe she's right. And I wonder if that's why I've found it all so hard, you know?'

Oscar's staring at me really intently and he looks so interested, so much like he really cares that I find I want to talk to him, I want to tell him what I've been thinking.

'I wonder if I'm sort of punishing him. Because he made things hard for me.' Oscar blurs in front of me as my eyes fill with tears.

'That sounds...reasonable,' he says, quietly.

'Really? It doesn't make me sound like a cow on wheels?'

Oscar laughs. 'No. Honestly, we're supposed to have this really healthy post-divorce family thing going on – and we have – but I was miserable when they first split up. I know it's better, but I just wanted them to work it out, you know? For me?'

'That's exactly what I said to Mum,' I tell him. I wipe my eyes with my thumbs. 'Ugh. Sorry.'

'Don't be sorry,' he says. And then he looks at my mouth. I may not have much experience, but I know what that means. He wants to kiss me. Oscar actually wants to kiss me. I try to think of something to say, but my mind's a total blank. All I can hear in my head is 'Oscar wants to kiss me?'

He glances up and looks right into my eyes and then his mouth is on mine and Oscar's kissing me. His mouth is soft and he smells so like Oscar that I almost feel we could be back in his old house with our parents downstairs playing Trivial Pursuit and arguing about the Hadron Collider.

My hands are hanging down at my sides and I don't know what to do with them, so I leave them there. I don't know where Oscar's hands are, but they're not touching me – the only part of us that's touching is our lips. I can't believe we're kissing. I think maybe we should stop.

I yank my head back too quickly and bang it on the bookshelves, actually knocking a book onto the floor.

'Emma, I—' Oscar starts.

'I'm sorry,' I interrupt. 'I didn't mean to—'

'No, I'm sorry. I didn't plan to do that or anything.' His cheeks and neck are mottled and red.

'It's OK. It just took me by surprise.'

'Are you all right?'

I put my hand up and wince as I touch what I assume is going to be a large bump right on the back of my head.

'I'll live,' I say. 'But...'

'...you need to go,' he finishes for me. He's still blushing and he can't quite meet my eyes, which is very unlike him.

'Yes. Sorry.'

I bend down to pick up the book that fell. It's Neil Gaiman's *Stardust*. Typical.

'Shall I walk you back?' Oscar says, taking the book out of my hands.

I shake my head. 'I'll be fine. Thanks.'

At the front door, he looks like he's going to say something else, but he looks confused and just tells me to take care.

'I will,' I say. 'Thanks.'

When I turn the corner, I look back, almost expecting him to be watching me go, but the door's closed and he's gone.

Chapter Fourteen

I phone Jessie before I even get home.

'So,' I say. 'Oscar kissed me.'

She gasps. 'He did not.'

'Yeah. He did.'

'And...how was it? Did you kiss him back? Where were you?'

I give her all the details and she says, 'Wow. Well I can't say I'm exactly surprised.'

'Why not?!'

'Oh, come on, Em! He always had a thing for you. He used to go all moony-eyed whenever you weren't looking.'

'He did not.'

'Yeah. He did. Is he still the same?' Jessie asks.

I turn the corner onto the canals. 'Sort of. He doesn't go moony-eyed if that's what you mean. He's just as dorky, but he's much more confident. He's funny too.'

'He was always funny.'

'Yeah, he was.'

'And you said he looks good, didn't you?' Jessie asks.

'Yeah, he does. His dress sense is a bit random, but...'

Jessie laughs. 'So why did you freak out when he kissed you?'

'I don't know! I just wasn't expecting it.'

'Are you waiting to hear from Alex Hall, is that it?'

I had emailed her after the Warner Brothers visit and she practically had us announcing our engagement on the cover of *People* magazine, but I haven't heard from Alex since.

'No. I don't think so. It was just...it's Oscar, you know?'

'I know,' Jessie says. 'But you shouldn't rule it out. Do you fancy him?'

I start walking over the bridge and realise I've actually passed the end of our road. I stop and lean on the railing. 'No. I don't know. I mean, I've never really thought about it.'

'Oh, come on,' she says. 'You totally have.'

I look at the palm trees reflected in the water. 'I didn't when he was at home, obviously.'

'Obviously,' she agrees.

'But now...he looks really good. He's funny and sweet and we get on well.'

'But there's no spark?'

I sigh. 'When I was talking to Alex I had butterflies. In fact, they were more than butterflies, I felt sick. I've never felt that with Oscar.'

'But...'

'But I think I did when he kissed me.'

'And it freaked you out,' Jessie says. She knows me so well.

'What if it didn't work out?' I say. 'We could hardly still be friends.'

'But what if it did work out? And don't forget you may not be able to be friends after this anyway,' she says.

'Oh, god. You're right. Unless we both agree never to mention it again?'

Jessie laughs. 'Yeah, that sounds healthy.'

'Ugh,' I say, smiling. 'You've been in New York too long.'

When I get home, I can't settle. I feel so restless that I even think about going for a run. And I don't run. Instead, I get the notebook I bought at Small World Books and take it out on the upstairs terrace.

I can't believe Oscar kept that moon drawing all this time. I remember exactly when I drew it. We'd been to Jodrell Bank Observatory with the school, which was a bit mad because my parents worked there. I bought a holographic postcard of the moon in the gift shop. At first, I was going to send that to Oscar, but then I decided to try and draw it myself. I did it on the coach on the way back to school, while everyone else was screeching and snogging and playing music on their phones. People thought I was being a bit weird, I know, but once I started, I couldn't stop. It was like I was in my own peaceful little bubble. That's exactly what I want right now.

I start drawing the potted palm tree in the corner of the terrace and everything else goes away. I get totally engrossed in recreating the leaves on the page and it's only when I've done it and I look up that I remember I'm sitting in the evening sunshine by the side of a canal in LA. While I was drawing, I could have been anywhere. Or nowhere.

Did I really stop drawing because Dad pushed me? I wish I could remember. I think about what Bex said – or what Bex said Dad said – that I give up on things too easily. I think it's a way of protecting myself, so I don't invest too much in something and then find it doesn't work out.

The light is flashing on my phone and I pick it up, expecting it to be Oscar, but it's a message from my dad: HOPE ALL IS OK OUT THERE. MISS YOU. HOPE WE CAN TALK SOON.

I turn my phone off.

Chapter Fifteen

'Emma. Emma. Emma. Emma!'

'Whaa?' I say, from under the quilt. What is it with LA and getting woken up at stupid o'clock? Why won't California let me sleep?

'You left your phone on the terrace,' Bex whispers.

'So?' I say. Or rather, groan.

'You've got a call. It's Alex Hall.'

'Rhymes,' I mumble and then realise what she said. Alex Hall. Is calling me. And I'm asleep. I reach my hand out from under the duvet and Bex puts my phone in it. I bring it back under the covers and take a deep breath.

'Hello?'

'Did I wake you?' he says. His voice sounds even nicer on the phone.

'No!' I say, trying to drag myself up on to my pillows.

Bex is bouncing up and down at the foot of my bed.

'I did, didn't I?' he says.

'Just a bit. What time is it?'

'Ten,' he says. 'I'm sorry. I'll let you go back to sleep.'

'No, no, honestly. It's fine. I need to get up anyway.'

'Oh. I just wondered. I was...' He pauses.

Is he actually nervous? Talking to me?

'OK,' he says. 'I've been running on the beach and I was just going to get breakfast and I wondered if you'd want to join me?'

'I've already eaten,' I say, smiling.

Bex pulls a 'WTF?' face.

'Right,' Alex says. 'Sure. Sorry. I shouldn't have phoned so early. I'll—'

'I'm joking,' I say. 'I'd love to come and meet you. Where are you?'

'Do you know the Starbucks on Washington?'

'Yes. I'll have to grab a shower so I'll be about half an hour, is that all right?'

'Cool,' he says. 'I'll do another couple of miles and see you there.'

I end the call and practically throw myself out of bed.

'I'll get in the shower, you find me something to wear,' I tell Bex. 'And can you google the quickest way to get to the Starbucks on Washington?'

She salutes and I fling myself into the bathroom.

Almost exactly thirty minutes later, I'm on Washington Boulevard, facing Starbucks and waiting for the lights to change. It was a really easy walk to get here – right along the main canal – but I still feel flustered. It's a bit much to be woken by a phone call inviting you on a date with a celebrity. Doesn't really give you much time to adjust to the idea.

I don't know if Alex can see me from inside the coffee shop, so I'm really conscious of crossing the road without falling over or otherwise making an arse of myself. Luckily the door says PULL so there's none of the pushing a pull door awkwardness. As soon as I'm inside, I see him. He's in the corner next to the window. He's got his phone in his hand, but he grins as soon as he sees me and stands up.

'Hi,' I say, brilliantly. All the way here I was trying to think of a fabulous opener, but it's just too early.

He reaches his hand out and then shakes his head and says, 'Ah, sorry – sweaty,' and wipes it on his T-shirt instead.

And he is pretty sweaty. He's wearing a white T-shirt and a grey beany hat and I can see that the ends of his hair are damp. He's got iPod headphones hanging around his neck.

I sit down opposite him and say, 'So you run on the beach?'

He nods. 'Not every day, but pretty often. Do you run?'

I laugh. 'No. I'm not a runner, no.'

'You should try it. It's pretty amazing.'

'Maybe I will,' I say. 'Climate change may make hell actually freeze over.'

He looks at me with a puzzled expression and then laughs. 'You're funny.'

I smile and try to think of something else to say, but my mind's blank. And then my stomach rumbles. Loudly.

'Oh god!' Alex says, and actually smacks himself on the forehead. 'Can I get you a drink? Something to eat?'

'That would be great, thanks,' I say. 'Can I have a latte? And...' I crane my head to look at the food, but I can't really see. 'What are you having?'

'I usually get a wrap,' Alex says. 'The spinach, feta and egg white's really good.'

I resist saying, 'Seriously?' and instead say, 'How about a muffin?'

'OK.' He stands up, but his headphones get caught on the back of the chair and ruck his T-shirt up, showing a thin strip of his stomach and, yes, washboard abs. I saw him completely shirtless last week, so I don't know why it gives me such a thrill, but there's just something about seeing a strip of stomach when someone's dressed. I've got dots in front of my eyes.

Once he's disentangled himself, Alex says, 'What flavour muffin?'

'Oh, I don't know,' I say. 'Surprise me.'

He grins and goes to the counter.

While I'm waiting I watch a woman outside trying to get a little dog to cross the road, but it's sitting down and refusing to budge. It's actually looking up at her with an expression on its face like 'Make me'. She tugs on the lead for a bit, but then gives up and just picks the dog up under her arm. It doesn't look impressed. I watch them as they cross the road and it's only when they walk out of my line of sight that I notice a man leaning against the wall opposite. He's dressed all in black including a back-to-front baseball cap and fiddling with the massive camera hanging around his neck.

Just as I'm shifting my seat so my back's to the window, Alex comes back. He puts two drinks and a muffin down on the table and sits down.

'I think that guy over there is paparazzi,' I say, pulling my latte towards me.

Alex glances over and says, 'Oh, yeah. He took some shots of me on the beach. He hangs around a lot.'

'Doesn't it bother you?'

He shrugs. 'Nah. It's part of the job.'

'It gives me the creeps,' I say. 'I'd never be able to properly relax.'

Alex pulls his hat off and runs his hand through his damp hair. 'You get used to it, honestly.'

I sip my latte and look at the muffin Alex brought. It looks unusual. 'What is this muffin?'

'Apple bran. Is that OK?'

'Great,' I say. But apple bran? Seriously? When there are chocolate muffins in the world? That's just wrong.

A female barista comes over and gives Alex his wrap, along with a flirty smile. I look at him, but he doesn't even seem to have noticed. It must be something else he's used to.

While we eat, he tells me how, just over a year ago, he moved to LA from Austin with his mum after his parents got divorced.

'I came out for pilot season – Mom said if I didn't get a job then we'd go home and I could try again when I was eighteen. But *Stellar Highway* was the third audition I had, so...'

'So you stayed?'

He nods. 'We went back and got a truck full of all our stuff and drove back.'

'Drove? Isn't it really far?'

'Fifteen hundred miles? Something like that. We took a few days. My mom likes a road trip.'

'That sounds really cool,' I say. 'We used to drive down to France, but my dad was really anal about it. Plotted the route down to the last mile. It wasn't exactly relaxing.'

He laughs. 'My mom's the opposite. I was worried we'd never get here. She was all for going to Vegas and the Grand Canyon.'

'So you got here, you got *Stellar Highway* and you never looked back?'

He grins. 'Something like that.'

'Is your dad still in Austin?' I ask.

He nods, his mouth full of food. Then he swallows and says, 'Yeah. We don't really talk.'

I think about how I'm not really talking to my dad at the moment either and I don't want to ask him anything else.

While we eat – the apple bran muffin actually isn't bad, but chocolate would have been so much better – Alex tells me some of the things Bex needs to watch out for at auditions.

'But Emily's great,' he says. 'She'll take care of her.'

'That's good to know,' I say. 'It's pretty scary to think she could get her own show and start having paparazzi waiting for her outside Starbucks.' I look out of the window – the guy's still there, but now he's talking on his phone.

'That's how you know you've made it!' Alex says. He drains the last of his drink and says, 'Have you got plans for today?'

I shake my head. 'Just hanging out at home with Bex. You?'

'I've got to go and do some press.'

'Oh, OK. Cool.'

We both stand and Alex walks around the table and opens the door for me. I follow him out into the street and notice the paparazzi guy straighten up and lift his camera. Alex puts his hand on my arm and steers me past the outside tables. At first I'm not sure what he's doing, but then I realise he's putting himself between me and the photographer.

'I'd walk you back,' he says, 'but he'll follow me now, so...'

'No, that's fine,' I say. 'This was really nice. Thank you for calling.'

'Sorry again for waking you up,' he says, and grins. His hand's still on my arm and I don't really know what to do. Is he expecting a kiss? I'm not sure I want to kiss him in front of the people sitting outside and particularly not with a photographer so near.

'So, I'll call you,' Alex says.

'Great.'

He glances back over his shoulder at the photographer, who is heading this way and then he turns and runs across the road. The photographer immediately chases after him, shouting his name.

I wait until Alex has got in his car, before crossing the road and walking back home.

Chapter Sixteen

I spend the rest of the day helping Bex with her recorded audition piece, sitting on the terrace, sketching, and checking my phone to see if Oscar's called.

I know I should phone him to make sure everything's all right between us, but I don't really know what to say. 'Sorry I freaked out and ran away when you kissed me'?

It doesn't help when Mum comes home and asks, 'How's Oscar?' like he's here all the time, like I see him every day.

And then Bex makes it worse by saying, 'Never mind Oscar – Emma had a date with Alex Hall this morning!'

I tell Mum all about it while we eat dinner and then I go up to the terrace to email Jessie.

I'm about halfway through what promises to be a mammoth email when I hear singing. It sounds like it's coming from the canal. It sounds like Oscar. I stand up and go over to the fence, holding on with both hands because it's pretty high up. I can't see him at first, but along with the singing – I can't tell what song it is yet – I can hear the sound of a paddle going through the water.

And then he appears. He's in a kayak and when he sees me he grins and waves. I'm surprised at how pleased I am to see him and his ridiculous, bright orange BAZINGA T-shirt.

'What are you doing?' I say, sheltering my eyes against the low sun.

'I'm sorry, Emma,' he sings, to the tune of 'O Sole Mio' – or 'Just One Cornetto' – 'for what I did. I wouldn't blame you, if you got rid. I know...I got your goat. But let's have noodles. At Wok the Boat!'

I shake my head. 'There's something seriously wrong with you,' I say.

He nods. 'I can't argue. Also, I can't claim to have written all of that song for this particular occasion. The last part I wrote for an ad. They never used it.'

'Shocking,' I say. I can't stop smiling.

He puts his hand up to his mouth as if he's speaking to me in an aside and says, 'So. You know. Are we cool?'

I nod. 'We're cool.'

'And your head's OK?'

'My head?'

'Where you, ah, banged it on my bookcase.'

Even from here I can see him blush.

'Oh,' I say. I bite my lip and then smile. 'I thought it was, but now I'm thinking this must be a hallucination brought on by a concussion.'

'You're not the first person to say that about my singing,' he says. 'I'll, er... I'll paddle off then.'

He tries to turn the kayak using one paddle, but just sort of flails about. It's utterly ridiculous. Eventually, he manages it and as he goes, says, 'Tomorrow night? Eight o'clock?'

'I'll be there,' I say. 'Brain damage permitting.'

He salutes and then, as he starts to paddle, tips a pretend hat and says, 'Bex. Mrs R.'

I'm still watching Oscar paddle away, badly, when I hear my mum call from downstairs:, 'Do you want to come down and tell us what that was all about?'

'I always knew he liked you,' Mum says. She hasn't stopped grinning since I told her about the kiss.

'That's what Jessie said,' I say. 'No one thought to mention it to me?'

'You really didn't know?' Mum says.

'No!' I say. 'And anyway, you heard him. He apologised. It's not like we're going out.'

'Are you mad?' Bex says. 'He just asked you out. And you said yes.'

I shake my head. 'He asked me to go to Wok the Boat, not on a date.'

'It's a date,' Bex says.

'Come on! It's not a date. He knows the kiss freaked me out and he wants us to go back to how we were. That was the point of the song!'

'I think the point of the song was to woo you,' Mum says, pouring herself a glass of wine.

'Woo!' Bex says, waving her hands in a bad ghost impression, and then laughs at her own crap joke.

'It was not!' I say. 'This is Oscar! He doesn't woo. Or at least he doesn't woo me.'

'So you're saying you're not interested?' Mum says.

I blow out a breath. 'I don't know. I hadn't really thought about it before. Much. But it's Oscar. He's my only friend here. I don't want to mess that up. You've always told me that friends are more important than boyfriends.'

'And they are,' Mum says. 'So boyfriends who are also friends are wonderful.'

'OK,' I say, 'but isn't it better to have a really good friend than a boyfriend who could change his mind and go off with someone else?'

'Oh, Emma,' Mum says. 'Don't let what happened between me and your dad affect you like that.'

I hadn't actually been thinking about Dad – I'd been thinking more of friends at school – but, of course, she's right, that's exactly what Dad did.

'You can't go into something worrying about how it's going to end,' Mum says. 'No one ever knows.

If you like someone, you have to take a chance. I'd hate to think you'd be so scared of getting hurt that you wouldn't risk being with someone.'

'No, I'm not, really,' I tell her. Although I'm not sure that's true.

'Is it because you like Alex Hall?' Bex asks. She's got her phone in her hand and a slightly evil grin on her face. No doubt she's texting her friends to tell them I've just been serenaded from a kayak.

'No,' I say. 'I mean, I do like Alex, but that's not why I'm not sure about Oscar.'

'You don't need to get serious with either of them,' Mum says. 'You can just see them both and work out how you feel.'

'I can't though, can I? I can't string Oscar along until I decide whether or not I'm really interested.'

'That's not what I said,' Mum says. 'I'm just saying it doesn't need to be so hard. You can just see them. As friends. And if you realise you want to take it further – with either of them – you cross that bridge when you come to it.'

'Ooh,' Bex says. 'Maybe they'll fight over you!'

I roll my eyes. 'That's so not going to happen.'

I don't know how this happened. The boys I like never like me, but now I've got my oldest friend and a proper Hollywood star interested? How am I supposed to deal with that?

Chapter Seventeen

I'm on my way to Wok the Boat when my phone rings. No number comes up, but I answer it anyway since sometimes calls from abroad come up that way.

A voice says, 'Emma?'

Sexy southern accent. Alex.

He says, 'Is this a good time?'

I head over to the little wall at the side of the path and sit down so I can concentrate. My arms feel weird, tingly.

I say, 'It's fine, yeah.'

'So I had a good time at breakfast yesterday.'

'Me too.'

There's a silence and I look up and down the path while I try to think of something to say. A barefoot woman who seems to be dancing to no music is heading straight for me, so I climb over the wall and walk on the sand.

'Did the press thing go well yesterday?'

'Yeah, it was fine, you know. Did more today. They all ask the same questions, so...'

'Right,' I say. I walk down towards the water.

'So what are you doing?'

'I'm just on my way to meet my friend Oscar,' I tell him. 'We're going to get noodles.'

'I like noodles,' Alex says. 'Where are you going?'

'Wok the Boat in Santa Monica. Do you know it?'

'I've passed it,' Alex says, 'but I've never been.'

'It's really good,' I say. 'You should go.'

'I'll add it to my bucket list,' he says and I laugh.

'So...' I say. I can see Wok the Boat from here.

'Yeah, I was just calling to see if you wanted to hang out,' Alex says, 'but obviously you're busy.'

'Right. Well, yeah. I'd love to. But no, not tonight.'

'Right.'

I stop and look back at the path. The woman is still dancing. 'Unless... I mean, you're welcome to join us, if you'd like to.'

'Your friend won't mind?'

I wiggle my feet down into the sand. 'No. He'd like to meet you, I'm sure.'

Alex says he'll see me there and I end the call and I stare at the phone. I just invited Alex Hall to come and hang out with me and Oscar. I put the phone back in my pocket, but I can't seem to make my legs move, so I take it out again, check the time and realise it's too late to call Jessie.

I walk down to the edge of the water and watch the tiny birds running in and out of the waves. As the water goes out, they run towards the ocean and then as it comes back in, they turn and run back up the sand. They do it over and over again.

I keep thinking about what my dad said about my drawing. That I gave it up to protect myself. Is that what I'm doing now? With Oscar? Am I really worried about losing him as a friend, or am I just scared of getting hurt? Because it would be so much worse to be hurt by Oscar than by someone like Alex. Because Oscar knows me. He's known me for most of my life. How can I take that risk?

And I like Alex, I really do. What I know of him. He seems funny and charming and of course he's so sexy. But I'm pretty sure I only invited him tonight because I'm scared to be alone with Oscar. What was I thinking?

When I get to Wok the Boat, Oscar's behind the desk taking an order. He grins at me and says, 'I won't be a minute.'

I hop up on a stool at one of the tables around the edge and flick through a copy of *US Weekly* someone left behind. Only a couple of pages in, there's a photo of Alex in the STARS – THEY'RE JUST LIKE US! section. He's putting petrol in his car and the caption says: STARS AND CARS! ALEX HALL PULLED OFF THE STELLAR HIGHWAY TO GRAB SOME GAS.

That's the other thing about Alex. If I go out with him, I have to deal with the paparazzi and the flirty baristas and everything else that comes with being a celebrity. Particularly here. I don't know if I could cope.

Oscar comes over and hops up on the stool next

to me. He's wearing the EXPELLIARMUS T-shirt I got him at Warner Brothers.

'I thought you had to wear a Wok the Boat shirt?' I say.

He looks down at his T-shirt. 'There was a small health-and-safety incident. Those flames can really leap.'

I frown. 'Listen,' I say, 'I need to tell you something.'

His eyes widen and I can tell he thinks I'm going to bring up the kiss. What I can't tell is whether or not he wants me to. I find myself glancing down at his mouth and force myself to look back up. 'I sort of invited Alex here.'

He blinks. 'Alex Hall? Now?'

'Yes. I'm really sorry. He phoned when I was walking over and when I said we were having noodles he said he likes noodles and then...'

He looks stunned. 'Wow. Er, OK. Yeah, that's no problem.'

'You really don't mind? I know I should've asked you first. I just didn't think.'

'No, that's fine.' He hops down off the stool and

says, 'I'd better warn the others. Don't want any embarrassing hysterical scenes. Sam's a screamer.'

I know as soon as the door opens that Alex has arrived. I hear the gasp from the other customers and actually feel the atmosphere change in the room. I look up and he's stopped just inside the door. He's wearing sunglasses and he's got his phone to his ear. When he sees me, he grins and I feel my stomach clench. On the one hand, I can't believe he's here to meet me. On the other, I still can't believe I invited him.

'Hey,' he says, hopping up on the stool next to me, where Oscar was sitting a little while ago. He smells fantastic, sort of woody with a bit of vanilla.

'You found it OK?'

He nods. 'I've run past it a few times, but I've never been in.' He grins. 'It's a crazy place. How are you?'

I tell him that I've spent the day helping Bex with her video audition and he says, 'I could come and read with her sometime, if she wants.'

'Seriously?' I say. 'That's so nice of you. She'd

love that. I think she's struggling a bit with doing it by herself, which is why I've been reading with her.'

'No problem,' he says. 'It does take some getting used to, but it's a really important skill to have. So many casting directors ask for videos now. Has she seen Emma Stone's *Easy A* audition? It's like a video masterclass.'

'I'll tell her. Thank you.'

'So what's good here?' Alex asks. He swivels on the stool to look at the menu up on the wall. He hasn't taken his sunglasses off.

Once his attention's off me, I realise that everyone else's attention is on him and I suddenly feel a bit self-conscious. So how weird must it be to be Alex? No wonder he wants to hide behind something.

'The pad thai's great,' I tell him. 'And the spring rolls are really good too.'

'Can we order?' he says. 'Or are we waiting for your friend?'

'Oh,' I say. 'He's here. I'll introduce you...'

As I look for Oscar, I feel slightly panicky. Everyone's looking at us and I don't know what I'm doing. It was a mistake to invite Alex tonight, I know it was. But it's too late now. Now I just have to get through it.

Tabby is standing at the counter, staring at Alex, an unfolded cardboard carton in her hands. Oscar's standing near the woks with a slightly puzzled expression on his face. As soon as I see him, I feel relieved.

'That's my friend Oscar in the dorky T-shirt,' I tell Alex.

Alex takes his sunglasses off, slides off his stool and heads towards the counter. Oscar comes round the front of the counter and shakes Alex's hand. 'The dorky T-shirt you bought me,' he says to me, smiling.

Something in his expression makes me think he said that on purpose to let Alex know what good friends we are, but Oscar's not like that. He wouldn't be possessive about me, I'm sure.

I introduce Alex to Tabby too and just as she's opening and closing her mouth like a fish, Sam appears through the back door. He says, 'What's shakin'?' and then stops dead, stares at Alex, and says, 'Holy sh— rimp! You actually came!'

'Good to meet you, man,' Alex says, holding out his hand to Sam.

'I *love* your show!' Sam grins and pulls Alex into one of those back-slapping hugs boys do.

Alex and I sit back down and Oscar sits on my other side. It's awkward because we're sitting at a bar, so we're all in a row. If I'm looking at Alex, my back is to Oscar and vice versa. I try to shuffle back a bit on my stool, but I'm too scared of falling off it backwards to go too far. I hold on to the edge of the bar, just in case.

Oscar asks Alex about his show and how long he's been in LA. He tells us about his audition for *Stellar Highway* and that his character's named Luke as a nod to Luke Skywalker and I see Oscar's face light up.

'I just read a brilliant blog post about watching the trilogies in a different order,' Oscar says. 'Apparently it works really well. If you skip *Episode I* altogether and start with—'

'I'm not really a *Star Wars* fan,' Alex interrupts, and I feel a bit taken aback on Oscar's behalf. God knows I don't want to sit here talking about Boba

Fett or whatever, but he could've at least let him finish his sentence.

Sam brings over the noodles and spring rolls and we spend a few minutes passing the boxes around and sharing the food out between us.

'What films do you like?' I ask Alex. 'If you're not a *Star Wars* fan.'

He leans on his elbow and rubs the back of his neck. 'I don't know. I really liked the Bourne films, you know? Matt Damon's a cool guy. Have you seen them?'

I shake my head. 'I liked him in *Ocean's Eleven*, though.'

Alex nods. 'Yeah, they were good. And I really like movies like *Captain America*, you know? *Thor*. *X-Men*. I'd love to do something like that.'

He and Oscar talk for a bit about *Captain America*, which I haven't seen, while I eat the spring rolls and look from one to the other, like I'm watching a tennis match.

Oscar is looking at Alex, but Alex is fiddling with his phone, looking around the room or down at his food. But I know that Oscar's eye-contact thing can be a bit hard to get used to so I can't really hold that against him. Not that I'm particularly looking for things to hold against him. At least, I don't think I am.

It's funny, if I'd thought about it before, I would have said they had nothing in common, looks-wise, but looking at them either side of me I realise they're actually quite similar-looking. They both have floppy fringes – although Oscar's is bright red and Alex's is brown with some very subtle highlights – and they both have really startling, huge smiles. Alex looks more polished and 'Hollywood' but they definitely have a look of each other. They've even got similar bluey-grey eyes. Weird.

Once they've exhausted the *Captain America* topic, Alex asks me about films and we talk about that for a while until Sam comes over with some more drinks.

'On the house,' he says, as he puts them down in front of us.

We thank him and he starts asking Alex about *Stellar Highway*. While Alex talks to Sam, I try to think of something to say to Oscar, but I can't think of a single thing apart from 'So. That kiss.' It's like an alarm blaring in my brain: KISS! KISS! KISS!

'I started drawing again,' I say, after a much longer silence than I've had with Oscar for a while.

His face lights up. 'Seriously? That's brilliant.'

'Yeah,' I say. 'It feels really good.' I'm about to say it was seeing the moon drawing in his room that made me want to try, but then I remember that I saw that drawing just before THE KISS so I grab a spring roll and shove it in my mouth instead.

'You waited for it to cool down,' he says, smiling. 'Progress.'

'I find you can appreciate the taste more if you haven't just seared the surface off your tongue,' I say. 'Tongue' is a bit closer to KISS than I'm really comfortable with, but it's too late now.

I look at Oscar out of the corner of my eye. He's pulling at his bottom lip with a finger and thumb. Is that a nervous thing or a dorky thing like locking his lips? I look up and realise he's just caught me looking at his mouth. I feel myself blush and swig my drink.

This is exactly what I was hoping to avoid with

Oscar. We've always been so comfortable together. Even after not seeing each other for years, we just fell back into our friendship so easily and I really liked that. It's exactly what I've missed since Jessie left. But Jessie's right, isn't she? The kiss has changed everything, whether we take it any further or not. So does that mean I may as well take it further? Does that mean I've got nothing to lose? Or does it mean I'm running the risk of losing Oscar either way?

One of the main tables becomes free when some people leave, looking back at Alex as they go, and we move over to sit there. I sit across from Alex and Oscar sits next to me. It's better than the bar because we don't have the awkwardness of sitting in a row, so the conversation flows better. Sam joins us for a while – until Tabby yells at him to get back to work – and I actually have a pretty good time, although I never manage to relax completely and I just can't stop comparing Oscar and Alex. It's exhausting.

Once we've finished all the food and drained our drinks, Alex says, 'I think I'd better head off. I've got an early call tomorrow, so...'

'Right,' I say. 'I should be getting back too, actually.'

'Can I give you a ride?' Alex says.

'Oh! That would be great, yeah. If you don't mind.'

He asks Oscar if he wants a lift too, but Oscar says he's going to stay behind and help Sam and Tabby clean up.

'You sure?' Alex says.

'Absolutely,' Oscar says, sounding really English in comparison to Alex, 'but thanks, man.'

I grin at the 'man' and Oscar pulls a face at me.

'Talk tomorrow?' I say and he nods.

I follow Alex towards the door, but just before we get there, a girl sitting at one of the other tables says, 'I love you, Alex' and darts forward to kiss his cheek as her friend snaps a photo on her phone. I think she calls me a bitch but I'm not sure. And then Alex opens the door and I'm blinded by flashes.

'Whoa!' Alex says from behind me. 'When did they turn up?'

He grabs my arm and tugs me to the left, along the front of the restaurant.

The paparazzi are shouting and the flashes and the clicking and whirring of cameras – there's even what looks like a TV camera there – are really disorientating.

Someone shouts 'Who's the girl, Alex?' and then it's all I can hear. They keep repeating it: 'Who's the girl, Alex?', 'Alex, what's her name?', 'What's your name, honey?'

Alex doesn't say anything to the photographers, but to me he says, 'Just keep walking. My car's not that far.'

The photographers follow us along the path and judging by the sound a few more people have joined in. It's quite frightening having them behind us – not looking round, just knowing they are there. My heart's racing. I don't like it at all. I see the car park ahead and then Alex clicks his key and I see the lights flash on his car: a huge, black SUV. I'm so relieved to get there. Once we're both in the car, Alex starts the engine and pulls away slowly, but the photographers are still clambering all over the car and the flashes are still going off from every direction. Alex just pulls through them all slowly, and then we're back on the main road and away from them all.

'Are you all right?' he asks me.

My hands are shaking. 'Yeah. Thanks. But that was horrible.'

'I'm sorry,' he says. 'I didn't know they were out there. One of them must have followed me from home.'

'It's not your fault,' I say. 'What do they even want? A photo of you coming out of a noodle place? Why?'

'Cos they can make a hell of a lot of money doing it,' Alex says.

'Yeah, I get that, but do they have to be so aggressive about it?'

'Like I said yesterday, you get used to it.'

'I don't know if I would want to,' I say.

We sit in silence for a couple of minutes and then Alex says, 'So Oscar's a nice guy.'

'He's great,' I say. And then I can't think of anything else to say, because he just is. He's really great. And I know I messed up really badly tonight.

We turn off Washington Boulevard and onto Oscar's street. I stare at his house as we pass, even though I know there's no way he can be home yet.

I tell Alex to turn right at the end of the road and he grins at me.

'Wow!' Alex says. 'You live here? On the canals? So cool.'

'Yeah,' I say. 'It is.'

We get to the end of my street and I say, 'You can just drop me here. If you go down there, you'll have to reverse out.'

'Are you sure? I can walk you down.'

'No, it's fine, honestly. Thanks, though.'

I open the door and the internal light comes on.

'Are you really OK?' Alex says. 'You seem freaked out.'

'I am a bit.' I smile at him. 'But I'll be fine after a good night's sleep.'

Alex looks concerned and, as I look at him, I realise something.

'Your eyes,' I say. 'They're different. I noticed earlier, but I wasn't sure...'

He pulls a face. 'I wear coloured contacts for the show. I'm supposed to have starlight in me or something. You thought they were real?'

I nod.

He grins. 'Nah. They're just for effect.'

'Right,' I say. 'Don't believe what you see on TV.'

I start to turn to get out of the car, but Alex says, 'Emma?'

When I turn back to face him, he leans forward and kisses me. My lips tingle, but I think it must be from the chillies in the pad thai because even though Alex Hall is kissing me, all I can think about is Oscar. I pull away and bang my head on the car door. What is with me and kissing? Is every kiss I ever have going to end in a potential concussion?

'Thank you,' I say, ridiculously. I almost run back to my house.

Chapter Eighteen

When I wake up, it takes me a while to shake off my dreams. I had the most terrible night's sleep. I kept dreaming I was back in Wok the Boat with the paparazzi outside, hammering on the windows, smashing their way in. I had it over and over again – it started the same each time, but the ending was different. Once the door burst open and the photographers flooded in, grabbing at Alex and me. Once I ran out of the back door with Oscar and we ran down to the beach and the water's edge. Once Alex and I drove away, but he just kept driving faster and faster until I screamed and then I woke up. It was exhausting.

Sitting up in bed, I switch my phone on and it rings almost instantly. Jessie.

'Have you seen TMZ?' she says straight away.

'No,' I say. 'Why?' But as soon as I say it I realise what it must be. 'Oh my god, really?'

'There are about ten photos and a video. Are you all right?'

'What does it say?'

'Nothing, really. Just WHO'S ALEX'S NEW GIRL? kind of thing. The video looks scary.'

'It was,' I say.

'But you're OK?'

'Yeah, I'm fine. Well, I'm freaking out, but I'm fine.'

'Why are you freaking out?'

I give Jessie all the details about last night. About how I panicked at the thought of being alone with Oscar and invited Alex along. About how it was weird between Oscar and me. About how I thought of Oscar when Alex kissed me. And about the kayak. She didn't even know about the kayak.

'You're such an idiot,' she says.

'Thank you. You're a good friend.'

'But, Em, it's obvious you like him!'

I kick the quilt off my legs; it feels claustrophobic.

'What am I going to do about Alex?'

'What do you want to do?'

'I can't cope with the paparazzi. I don't want to be on TMZ.'

'You need to tell him that, then.'

'Yeah,' I say. I swing my legs off the bed. My head is banging.

'Listen,' Jessie says. 'I've actually got something that might cheer you up.'

'Oh, good,' I say. 'Spill it.'

I slide open the door and step out onto the terrace. The wood is warm under my bare feet.

'Mum's got a meeting in LA next week,' Jessie says. 'And she suggested I fly out with her—'

I screech so loud that a few small birds actually fly up off the fence and flutter in a panic.

After I've showered and had some breakfast and Bex has tried to convince me to do some yoga with her because, according to her, I 'look really wound up', I phone Oscar, but it goes straight to voicemail.

I leave a message apologising for inviting Alex along and for all the paparazzi turning up at Wok the Boat and asking him to call me. I really wish I could speak to him. It seems wrong leaving a message, but it also seems wrong not to leave one.

I stare at it for a while, willing Oscar to phone back and then I notice I've got a voicemail. From Alex. He apologises for the TMZ thing and says, 'I know it was a lot to deal with last night. And now this. I'm really sorry. I didn't mean to freak you out. Give me a call.'

I sit on the terrace and sketch for a while until the tiredness from the disturbed night's sleep catches up with me and I fall asleep.

When I wake up there's a text from Oscar: NO PROBS. WE'RE COOL. PLEASE DON'T COME ROUND SINGING ;-)

I smile at the phone. I'm glad he's all right. I'd be stupid to risk losing a friend like him.

I phone Alex and am surprised when he answers almost immediately.

'I'm so sorry about the paparazzi stuff,' he says, again.

'I know, that's OK,' I tell him.

'I forgot what it feels like the first time it happens

to you. Then when I saw that video this morning... you looked scared.'

'It was scary. But I'm fine now. Don't worry.'

'You looked pretty scared when I kissed you too,' Alex says.

I picture his face and I smile. 'I'm really sorry about that. I...I can't cope with the paparazzi stuff. I'm sorry, but I just wouldn't be able to relax.'

'That's OK,' he says. 'Thanks for being honest with me.'

'No problem,' I say and then I feel terrible. Because I haven't been honest at all, have I? With anyone.

Chapter Nineteen

Mum's gone straight from work to get her hair cut and Bex and I are meeting her for dinner at the Sidewalk Café. We get there a bit early so we walk over to the skatepark. I've brought my notebook, so I sit on a low wall next to the multi-coloured VENICE ground mosaic, while Bex leans over the skatepark railings. I draw the lifeguard hut on the beach and when I'm done, I look over and see Bex talking to the boy whose skateboard got loose when we were talking to Tabby. I walk over.

'This is Drew,' Bex says. He's quite cute with shaggy hair and skinny jeans. 'He says he can teach me to skate.'

'Brave boy,' I tell him and he grins.

'It's a good thing to have on your résumé,' he says. He's got a surprisingly deep voice.

'Drew's been in *Zeke & Luther*,' Bex tells me and I roll my eyes. Of course he has.

Bex and I are walking back across the grass to the Sidewalk Café when I hear someone shout, 'Hey! Emma!'

I turn round and see Tabby heading straight for me. She looks so furious that for a second I think she's going to hit me, but she stops dead in front of me and says, 'What's your problem?'

'What?' I can't quite believe this is happening.

'You heard me. What's your problem? Oscar's a great guy and you bring Alex Hall along on a date?'

'It wasn't a date. We're just friends. Not that it's any of your business.'

'It's my business because Oscar is my friend. And you – you're supposed to be his oldest friend. He was so excited about you coming to live over here – you treat him like crap.'

'I don't,' I tell her. 'Things have been a bit weird the last couple days, but I've spoken to him and he knows I'm sorry about the Alex thing.'

She shakes her head and starts to walk away, but then turns back. 'You're clueless. You don't deserve him.'

Bex and I get a seat outside the Sidewalk Café. The family at the next table has tethered their dog to the railing – the dog is on the boardwalk side – but he keeps jumping up so they can feed him bits of their breakfast.

'Are you OK?' Bex asks, for at least the third time. I've told her I don't want to tell Mum about Tabby and she agreed not to mention it.

I nod. 'She doesn't know what she's talking about. I apologised and he texted and he's fine. Everything's fine.'

Bex tries to distract me by telling me about an audition Emily's planning to send her on and, as she talks, I watch the people on the Boardwalk. There's the rollerblading electric-guitar turban guy we see every time and then a girl appears wearing tiny gold shorts, a gold bikini top and cowboy boots. She stands for a second as if she's thinking of coming in to the café, but then backflips away down the Boardwalk as if it's the most natural thing in the world.

Mum arrives just as the gold girl disappears out of view.

'Did you see that?' she asks, laughing.

'Your hair looks fantastic,' I say. It's much shorter, just about shoulder-length, with a sweeping fringe and she's had it coloured too, to a sort of honey blonde.

'It makes you look about twenty years younger!' Bex says, which is a bit of an exaggeration since Mum's forty-two and she certainly doesn't look twenty-two. She does look lovely though, the best I've ever seen her look.

She's had the same hairstyle for pretty much her entire adult life – there are photos of her with Dad at university and Mum's hair was the same: long, mousy brown, mostly straight but curly towards the ends. The only thing that's ever changed is that she's started to get the odd grey hair at the sides. This cut – and especially the colour – really is a transformation.

'Well, I need to look my best for the fancy benefit we're all going to,' Mum says.

'What's this?' I ask.

'It's at the Griffith Observatory. It's going to be very glamorous. There'll be all manner of celebrities and beautiful people there. And we're all going.'

Bex bounces in her seat and starts asking about the dress code, while I stare at a man walking past with his skin painted red, wearing a loincloth and dragging a huge wooden cross.

'This place is insane,' I say.

'You can't call it boring, though,' Mum says. 'And I don't know about you, but I'm more than ready for a bit of excitement in my life.'

'Really?' I say. 'You were bored at home?'

Before she can answer, the waiter comes over to take our order.

I think one of the reasons I found the past year so hard is that life had become so uncertain. Before they split up, even though my parents worked a lot, they were always really dependable. Even when I was sympathising with Jessie for her mum leaving and moving to New York, and for her dad falling in love with another man, I was also a bit envious. Jessie's family was interesting, at least. Mine were always just a bit...beige. But then when my dad fell in love with someone else and left and we had to sell the house, beige started to seem preferable.

'It's not so much that I was bored,' Mum says, once the waiter's gone. 'I'd arranged my life exactly how I wanted it, which was fine. But then there were no surprises. Ever. I got stuck in a rut, I suppose. Your dad and I both did. At first it's comfortable and then, after a while, it just becomes routine and it's so hard to break out of.'

'So if Dad hadn't met Clare...?'

'Who knows?' she says. 'Maybe we'd have ended it anyway. Maybe I would have met someone.'

'We always thought you were happy,' Bex says.

Mum reaches over and takes my sister's hand. 'We were! We were really happy for a long time. And then even when we weren't exactly happy, we weren't unhappy either. I know it was a shock to you when your dad and I split up. God knows, it was a shock to me too. But he was right to leave. Maybe not the way he did it, but he was still right.'

'How can you say that?' I say. 'You could've worked it out. You could've gone to counselling or something. He didn't have to just leave.'

Mum shakes her head. 'Sweetie, we did go to counselling. We just weren't in love any more.'

'You went to counselling? When?'

'We went a few times over the past few years. We tried really hard to make it work. The last thing we wanted to do was split up the family.'

'It might have been the last thing *you* wanted to do, but it obviously wasn't the last thing Dad wanted to do,' I say. I look at Bex. She looks tearful.

'You really should give your dad a break, Em,' Mum says. 'I know how much it hurt you when he left. It broke his heart. But what did you want him to do? He's happy with Clare. Would you rather he was unhappy with us?'

'Yes,' I say, forcefully. 'Because it's not just about him. What about us? Doesn't he care about our happiness?'

'Of course he does. But not at the expense of his own. And that's absolutely right. I think I'd have done the same, if I'd met someone.'

'You wouldn't,' I say.

'You don't know that, Em,' Mum says. 'You don't

know what you'd do until you're in that situation. All I know is that your dad loves you two more than anything. He always has and he always will.'

When Mum goes inside to pay, Bex says, 'Don't you think you'll ever forgive Dad?'

The question catches me off-guard and I actually gasp.

'I mean, he didn't do it to hurt you,' Bex says. 'He just fell in love with someone else.'

My eyes fill with tears. I remember telling Jessie that her mum hadn't taken up with Ben to hurt her – she'd just fallen for him. It's so easy to give advice to other people and so hard when it happens to you. Ugh.

I sigh. 'Of course I will.'

'So why don't you phone him?' she says. 'He asks about you every time I talk to him. He really misses you.' The two red patches rise on her cheeks and, for a second, it makes me think of Oscar.

'I miss him too,' I say. 'I'm just not ready to talk to him yet.'

Bex nods. 'Can I tell him that?'

My sister is so much wiser than she seems. 'Yes. You can tell him that.'

We decide to walk up to Santa Monica. Mum hasn't seen the pier yet and Bex wants another go on the Ferris wheel.

We're about halfway when I see a flash of Oscar's distinctive red hair in the distance and my stomach flips over.

'Is that Oscar?' Mum says, squinting into the sun. 'It is. I would never have thought he'd be one for hair like that, you know. He was always so shy.'

'He's changed a lot,' I say. 'I'm amazed at how much, really.'

He's busking near the Hot Dog Stick place and a few people are standing around listening. Some tourists are even taking photos.

'He's good,' Mum says, smiling.

And he is. He's really good. I don't know the song – I don't know if it's a real song or something he's written himself – but he's singing it confidently and smiling his huge smile. And then he turns our way and falters for just a second, before raising one eyebrow and getting right back into the swing of it. The crowd seems to love him and it's not hard to see why.

When he finishes the song, he says, 'I'm just going to take a quick break. Back in two.'

He reaches down and picks up the bag that had been between his feet and I realise it's heavy with change.

'You're really good!' Mum says.

'You mean you didn't think my kayak song was my best work?' Oscar says, grinning.

'Well, that was wonderful, of course,' Mum says, smiling at me. 'But I think this one was even better. Did you write it?'

He nods. 'It's called "Love on the Box". It's based on the Neil Diamond song, "Love on the Rocks", but it's about falling in love with a TV character.'

Mum and Bex both laugh, but I immediately feel paranoid. Does he mean me? Or am I just being completely egotistical? And Alex isn't a TV character, of course, he's a TV actor. But still. Maybe Tabby's right and Oscar isn't quite as OK with things as I assumed.

Chapter Twenty

I haven't told Jessie I'm meeting her at the airport, but her mum, Natalie, knows. I had to confirm the times with her and make sure I was OK to travel back in the car with them. She and Jessie have got separate, adjoining rooms at their hotel, so Natalie's arranged for me to stay overnight with Jessie. I'm so excited I can barely stand still. I can't quite believe it's been a year since I last saw her. She was supposed to come back to Manchester for Christmas, but then her dad surprised her with a trip to Barbados after he and Rhys got married, so she didn't make it back. We've Skyped and talked a lot, but it's not the same.

I see Natalie first and she spots me – she's

obviously looking out for me. She smiles and winks and then carries on talking to Jessie as if nothing's up. They both look fantastic. Natalie is as glamorous as always – she'll fit in very well in LA – and Jessie looks great too. Her long hair is tied back in a low ponytail and she's wearing jeans and a hoodie with the logo of her mum's Broadway show on it. I'm glad things have improved so much between them. I always really liked Natalie, but she and Jessie have had to work hard to become as close as my mum and I have always been. I sometimes forget how lucky I am. Actually, I often forget how lucky I am.

Jessie spots me and looks a bit confused for a second before she bursts out laughing and runs over to me. We hug and jump up and down and squeal a bit. People look over and laugh.

'It's so good to see you!' I say.

'You too!'

Natalie puts an arm around each of us and says, 'It's so lovely to be here. Emma, you look wonderful. LA suits you.'

'Oh, I don't know about that,' I tell her.

'It does!' Jessie says. 'You look much more

relaxed. Are you even wearing make-up?'

I wrinkle my nose. 'Not really. I tinted my eyelashes so I don't need to bother. It just melts in the sun anyway.'

Jessie laughs. 'From the girl who was never without a lip gloss! I'm shocked!'

'Well, you look wonderful on it,' Natalie says, leading us over to a nearby Starbucks. 'I need a coffee and then we'll go straight to the hotel.'

She orders a black coffee for herself and Jessie and I both get Frappuccinos. While we're waiting to collect them, Natalie phones the 'car service' and, by the time the coffees are done, there's a car waiting for us out front.

'You didn't want the authentic LA experience?' I ask, smiling. When Jessie and I arrived in New York, Natalie had us take a taxi rather than a car because, according to her, it was 'more authentic'.

'Oh, a town car *is* the authentic LA experience, darling,' Natalie says, smiling.

The car is luxurious without being over the top. As the driver pulls away from the airport, Jessie looks out of the window. 'Palm trees!'

I laugh. 'I think that's one of the first things I said too. It's weird seeing them at an airport.'

'So how are you enjoying it so far?' Natalie asks me.

'It's actually really great. It still seems ridiculous that this is my life now – I keep thinking I'm on holiday – but Mum and Bex are really happy and I've started to get used to the sun and everything.'

'It sounds like it's going really well for Bex,' Jessie says.

I nod. 'It's amazing actually. She's been working with Emily, her agent, on how to present herself at auditions and that kind of thing. As soon as a part comes up that Emily thinks she's right for, she's ready to go for it. She's really excited about it all, obviously.'

'That's so fantastic,' Natalie says.

'You never know,' Jessie says. 'She may end up appearing in Mum's film.'

I laugh, shaking my head. 'How mad is this? You writing a screenplay and Bex with an agent!'

Natalie grins at me. 'You have to go after your dreams. I told you two that in New York.'

'You did,' I say. 'I'm still struggling, though.'

'Are you?' Natalie says, frowning. 'Even in LA?'

'LA's made it worse. It's given me more options. And made me question the ones I had back in Manchester.'

'Well, that's good,' Natalie says. 'Questioning is good. And you don't need to make immediate decisions, do you? You've got plenty of time.'

'For most of them, yes,' I say. 'Anyway, never mind that. Tell me about New York. And this screenplay!'

'Oh, New York is amazing,' Natalie says. 'The show's still going really well.'

'How's Ben?' I ask.

She doesn't say anything, just holds out her left hand to show me the enormous diamond ring on her fourth finger.

'Oh, wow!' I say, grabbing it. 'Congratulations!'

'Thank you. We're really happy.'

I look at Jessie, who rolls her eyes, but she's smiling too.

Jessie tells me about her school as we drive through LA – stopping every now and then to gawk out of the window.

'Have you seen the Hollywood sign?' she asks, spotting a sign directing us to Hollywood.

'Yes,' I tell her, 'but only from pretty far away. You're not allowed to go up there any more. People kept changing the letters or hanging things from it for different protests.'

'That's a shame,' Natalie says. 'A starlet committed suicide off the H, you know? In the 20s.'

'Wow,' Jessie says. 'What a way to go.'

'Yep,' Natalie says. 'She got the celebrity she craved in death, rather than in life. People will do anything to be famous in this town.'

I nod, thinking about Alex. Being chased through the streets by paparazzi is a hell of a price to pay for fame.

Natalie asks about my parents and I'm still telling her about Mum's apparent LA transformation when the car pulls into the hotel car park. They're staying in a hotel right on the beach and only about ten minutes' walk from us, which is fantastic.

'The studio originally suggested The Standard,' Natalie says, when I comment on the hotel. 'But I didn't want to stay somewhere quite so scene-y, you know? And who can resist the beach?'

. The rooms are gorgeous: huge and bright with a balcony overlooking the beach. Natalie tells us she's going for a bath and to settle ourselves in and we do – kicking off our shoes and curling up on one of the huge beds with Cokes and crisps from the minibar.

'So,' Jessie says. 'Tell me everything.'

And I do.

Chapter Twenty-one

Oscar is waiting for us at the Sidewalk Café and he stands up when we arrive. I'm surprised at how pleased I am to see him, but I'm nervous because I have no idea how he's feeling about things. Or how I'm feeling about things. Talking to Jessie helped a lot, but I'm still confused.

He and Jessie aren't quite sure how to greet each other – they haven't seen each other for a few years and they weren't really friends, they were each just my friend – but they eventually go for a loose hug and then we all sit down.

'So did you two get any sleep at all?' Oscar asks, grinning.

'Not really,' I say. 'We talked pretty much all night.'

Oscar orders a Coke and Jessie and I both order lattes in an attempt to stay awake for the rest of the day.

'This place is fantastic,' Jessie says, staring out at the Boardwalk.

'Segways!' I almost yell as a Segway tour goes past.

Jessie laughs. 'We're not doing that.'

'Oscar wants to do it,' I say.

Oscar rolls his eyes. 'I don't,' he tells Jessie. 'It's a bit Emma's trying to make happen.'

I grin at him. 'I'm going to try "the first one to spot them doesn't have to pay".'

'I'm going to book her on it one of these days,' he tells Jessie. 'See how she likes that.'

We order some food – Jessie and I were so busy talking last night, that we hardly ate anything but mini-bar peanuts and we're both starving – and while we're waiting, Oscar and Jessie chat while I mainly think about how tired I am.

Jessie tells Oscar about the college courses she's

thinking of taking and he tells her about his plans to be an astronaut. She doesn't even laugh.

'Wow,' Jessie says. 'That's really impressive. I really hope you make it.'

'Now why couldn't you have said something like that?' Oscar asks me. 'Instead of taking the piss?'

'I can't help it,' I say. 'I was born this way.'

The food arrives and we dig in, watching the world go by on the Boardwalk. A guy playing the piano has a cat with him and the cat seems to be waiting until he's engrossed in playing before attempting a slow and sneaky escape. But she only gets a few metres away before the guy realises, stops playing, goes after her, picks her up and takes her back to the piano. And then the whole thing starts again.

'Is the piano here all the time?' Jessie asks.

Oscar's just taken a bite of his burger, so he shakes his head and points to his mouth. Once he's swallowed, he says, 'No, he wheels it on and off the Boardwalk. He must live nearby though, cos it takes about four people to push it.'

I tell Oscar that Mum and Bex have gone with Emily to meet with a casting director to talk about a Disney movie. It's exactly what I joked that Bex would want before we came here. I can't believe it's really happening, although it's Bex, so I sort of can.

Jessie asks me where the bathrooms are and I point to the back right corner of the bar. She gets up and heads inside. And it's only after she's gone that I realise Oscar and I are alone. I stare out at the Boardwalk. Two little blond boys go past wearing wetsuits and carrying small surfboards – they don't look older than ten, but they do look incredibly confident with their sea-tousled hair and boards under their arms.

'So,' Oscar says.

I look at him. 'So...'

'How's Alex?'

A woman goes past on a skateboard. She's holding the lead of a Great Dane and letting the dog pull her along.

'I'm not...seeing him. Any more.'

'Right. Is that your choice or...?'

I look at him. 'Yes. My choice.' I take a deep breath. 'I'm really sorry I invited him that night...'

He does a kind of shooing motion with his hands

and says, 'Meh. Let's never speak of it again.'

And then Jessie comes back.

When we've finished lunch, we start walking towards Santa Monica. It's odd to be introducing Jessie to the Boardwalk and laughing at her excitement. We walk across the sand to the water's edge and watch the tiny birds – sanderlings – run towards the waves and then desperately back up the sand to escape them. They look like children playing What's the Time, Mister Wolf?

Jessie takes a photo of the three of us and sends it to Finn. By the sound of it, things are going brilliantly with him. I really would love to have what Jessie and Finn have. I ask her to send a copy of the photo to me too and I feel my phone vibrate in my pocket when she does.

Further along the beach, we stop for a little while to watch the surfers and then we see a dolphin jumping over the crest of a wave.

'Oh my god!' Jessie yells. She spends the next five minutes training her phone on the waves to try to get a photo of it. We see the dolphin a few more times, but she doesn't manage to catch it.

'I love New York,' she says, as we walk along the sand, 'but I have to say I envy you guys living here – it's pretty cool.'

'You'll have to come back,' I say. 'And bring Finn.'

'I definitely will,' she says. 'Mum seems to think she'll be coming back too, so maybe we'll come with her.'

'That would be fantastic,' I say.

Oscar decides to walk up to Third Street Promenade with us and busk up there. On the way, he tells us everything he knows about the benefit at the Griffith Observatory. Jessie and Natalie are coming too now – Natalie bought tickets – and it sounds like it's going to be pretty fancy. It's to raise research funds for a study on the evolution of stars.

'I have no idea what that means,' I tell Jessie. 'Although Mum has tried to tell me.'

'OK,' Oscar says, 'so you know that stars form in the coldest regions of molecular clouds, right?'

Jessie and I look at each other. He may know this. We do not.

'But we don't really understand the environment or the evolution of the clouds,' Oscar continues.

'And why do we need to?' I ask him. I'm not being entirely facetious – although I am a bit – I genuinely don't understand the relevance of my parents' studies.

'Well, imagine the molecular clouds are LA,' Oscar says as we pass the gymnastics rings and stop for a minute to stare at the men swinging and flinging themselves around apparently effortlessly.

'We've got a world full of celebrities – stars – and we know where they came from. We know the films are made in LA. We know how and why LA got to be the centre of the movie industry, and we know the weather's great. But with real stars, we don't know any of that. We've just got the stars.'

'So it's as if, say, Angelina Jolie just suddenly appeared out of the blue?' Jessie asks.

'Sort of,' Oscar says. 'But not really. It's not the best analogy. They'll explain it to us when we go over to UCLA.'

Mum and Michael have invited us over to have a look at the research so we understand what the benefit is in aid of.

'It's better than Mum managed,' I tell Oscar,

smiling, 'but I still don't really understand why it's so important to know about stars. Isn't there more important stuff on earth they should be studying?'

Oscar points to the beach. 'Well, you know there are more stars in the universe than grains of sand on earth, right? Think about that. How can it not be important? We have no idea yet of the scale of the universe, but we know that it's full of stars. And of course, the sun is a star – you don't think it's important for us to understand the sun?'

I scuff some sand with the toe of my flip-flop and shake my head. This is why I was never interested in what Mum and Dad were doing – it makes my brain hurt.

Third Street Promenade looks more like a film set than a real shopping street. It's pedestrianised with palm trees down each side and little Parisian-style stalls and cafés in the middle. It's very stylish and incredibly clean.

'You're shopping, right?' Oscar says. 'I'll walk up to the top and you'll find me there when you're done.'

'We'll bring you a coffee,' Jessie tells him.

On the way into Sephora, we pass a tall, blonde woman pulling two small children in a red Radio Flyer wagon. I elbow Jessie because I think it might actually be Heidi Klum, but she's passed us by then and we can't tell from the back.

After Sephora, we weave in and out of shops all the way up the street. It actually doesn't take us that long to find dresses for the benefit. There's an amazing selection here and the staff are all unfailingly polite and helpful. My dress is navy blue with silver sparkles. It's got a V neck and a slightly flared skirt and I love it. Jessie's is black with a lace overlay top. It's so perfect for her that she could have designed it herself. She keeps peeking into the bag to look at it. We get shoes and underwear and then finally reach the end of the street and Oscar.

He's singing a song that seems to be about the periodic table, but the way he's singing it, it sounds like a dramatic love ballad. Once again, people are transfixed.

'He's really good, isn't he?' I say.

'You two are killing me,' Jessie whispers.

I look at her and she grins.

'What?'

'You're so made for each other.'

I snort. 'Hardly. When he was talking about stars back there, I barely understood a word.'

'It doesn't matter. It's like that when Finn talks about architecture. I've no idea what he's going on about, but I love listening to him.'

I stare at Oscar. Things have been fine between us today, which makes me think we could get past the kiss. We could go back to being just friends. And now that I know it's possible, I don't know if that's what I want.

'I cocked up so badly after he kissed me,' I say to Jessie. 'I don't even know if he'd still be interested.'

Jessie puts her arm around me. 'He serenaded you from a kayak, Emma. He's interested.'

Chapter Twenty-two

The UCLA campus is really beautiful: green and leafy with loads of the terracotta buildings we saw from the coach.

'Do you know where you're going?' I ask Oscar, who's slowed the car down to about five miles an hour.

'Not exactly,' he says, squinting out of the windscreen. 'I can never quite remember. All the buildings look the same!'

I roll my eyes. 'I knew I should've got Mum to write directions down for us.'

'You worry too much,' Oscar says. 'I'll find it in just a minute. How hard can it be?'

'People are staring at us,' Bex says, from the back seat, where she's sitting next to Jessie.

She's right. I don't know whether it's because we're going so slowly that we're almost stationary or they've just never seen a VW Beetle that looks like a giraffe before, but the students on either side of the road are definitely staring at us. Some of them are laughing. One guy actually takes a picture of us on his phone.

'Did you see that?' Oscar says. 'I don't know what's wrong with some people.'

I suggest I phone Mum and get her to talk us in.

'I won't be defeated!' Oscar says.

'Oh, please. Not that old "men don't ask for directions" chestnut,' I say.

'You're right,' Oscar says. 'I'm comfortable with my feminine side. Please phone her.'

I ring Mum and it turns out we're actually just a couple of turns away from her building, which is low and pure white in contrast to all the terracotta.

Oscar parks outside and says, 'Ta-da!'

'Ta-da what?' I say. 'If it was up to you we'd still be conducting the world's slowest safari out there.'

'I did it on purpose,' he says. 'To make you feel useful.'

'Can you two stop bickering?' Bex says. 'You're like an old married couple.'

I look at Oscar and see his cheeks have gone pink so I know he's thinking of us as a couple, same as I am.

Mum appears at the door, waving, and we all follow her up to her office. It's actually really lovely, with large windows overlooking a quad outside. It's much nicer than her office was in Manchester – that only had a tiny window high up on the wall and constantly flickering strip lights.

'So this is where I spend eighty per cent of my time,' Mum says.

Michael appears from another room.

'What's through there?' Oscar asks. 'Napping suite?'

'It's not quite that fancy,' Michael says, grinning. 'Just the kitchen. I don't think it had been put in last time you were here, had it?'

Oscar goes with his dad to make coffees for everyone and Mum shows me, Jessie and Bex what she's been working on. At first, she shows us a few diagrams and talks about 'young stellar objects' and 'protostars' and I feel the same way I've always felt, that I'm just not going to get this. But then she mentions molecular clouds.

'Oscar was telling us about them,' I say. 'He said they're like LA.'

Mum laughs. 'In that they're where stars are made? Nice analogy. I'll show you an animation.' She clicks around her computer apparently randomly and I stare in awe. It's a while since I've been to see Mum at work and I'd forgotten how confident and comfortable she is there. I've been worrying at how she's changed physically since we've been here – her new hair and manicures and white teeth – but I hadn't really thought about how completely in her element she is at work. All that stuff's just cosmetic. This is the part of Mum that really matters and it's the part I've been ignoring all these years. I can be such an idiot.

Mum finds the animation and it starts to play as Michael and Oscar come back in with coffees and Cokes for us all.

The animation starts with a bright dot with what looks like a tornado on each side. Everything is spinning and there's a disc of what looks like dust spinning around the dot too. As it spins and spins, the dot gets bigger.

'So that's a molecular cloud?' I ask.

Mum nods. 'And that's what forms the star.' She points to the dust disc. 'It attracts the surrounding gas and dust that creates its mass, actually becomes the star.'

This is when Mum usually loses me, when she starts talking about gas and dust and mass, but I'm still staring at the animation and it's strangely beautiful.

'So the star is made of dust?' I ask.

She nods. 'And gas, yes.'

'What does "we are all made of stardust" mean?' I ask Oscar.

'What?' He goes a bit pink.

'I saw it on a badge on your bag. I've heard it before, but I've never really thought about it. What does it mean?'

'It means what it says,' Oscar says, pulling his

bag up on his lap and looking along the strap for the badge. 'The carbon, nitrogen and oxygen atoms in our bodies were created in the stars.'

'But what does that mean?' I say. I've got a strange feeling in my stomach. I swig some Coke.

'It means we're all made of stars,' Oscar says.

'All the matter in the universe is essentially made of heavy elements that were created in previous generations of stars,' Michael says. 'Billions of years ago. When a star dies, the material disperses through space and goes on to be part of subsequent stars and planets. And people.'

I look at the animation again. 'Well, that's just ridiculous,' I say.

'I told you it was fascinating,' Oscar says, grinning.

'Me too,' Mum says, and squeezes my hand.

All the way home I think about the star animation. Stars are like people and people are actually made of stars. Stars are created by attracting everything around them and that's how people are created too. Isn't it? Everything spins around us and becomes part of us, whether it's music, TV, films, skateboarding, even other people. We take it all on and it becomes part of how we define ourselves.

So for my parents and for Oscar it's astronomy. For Bex it's acting. For Alex I suspect it might be fame. I'm not exactly sure what it's going to be for me right now or in the future, but I do know what made me the person I am today.

'Are you all right?' Oscar asks.

'No,' I say. 'I think I might be broken.'

He laughs. 'I know what you mean. It's mind-blowing. But it's endlessly fascinating. There are so many parallels with, you know, life.'

'That's what I was just thinking about,' I say. 'It's the parallels that are making my head hurt.'

'Why do you think humans have been fascinated by stars for so long?' Oscar says.

'I just thought it was because they twinkle,' I say, and grin at him.

When we get home, I go out on the upstairs terrace and pull a chair over towards the fence. Not close enough so I'm looking down, but close enough that I can put my feet on one of the wooden rails and look over at the houses on the opposite bank and up into the trees. It's warm and quiet and I've only been sitting there for a few minutes when a bird lands on the top of the fence. It looks like a sparrow. I haven't seen a sparrow here before; it's like a tiny bit of home. The bird turns around, hopping from foot to foot, sees me, cocks its head and flies away.

I can't stop thinking about how we're all made from everything around us. How our experiences and the people in our lives literally make us the people we are. And I like the person I am. Most of the time.

Since Dad left, I've tried really hard not to think about the good memories I have from before he left. Like how he used to take me outside in my pyjamas to show me the moon. How if I went in his office when he was working, he'd always stop what he was doing – no matter how important it was – and ask me about my day. How he used to watch *Friends* with me, even though he didn't really like it. How he talked Mum into letting me go to New York with Jessie, because he said it would be an incredible experience.

And I think about how Mum said they'd fallen out of love. How they'd tried to stay together, but eventually realised they'd be happier apart. But mainly I just think about how much I miss him. Have been missing him since the day he left.

I take out my phone, scroll through to DAD and press CALL.

Chapter Twenty-three

The road to Griffith Observatory is steep and winding and lined with trees, giving it a slightly magical air.

Mum and Michael got there early as hosts and Oscar went with them, so Bex and I have travelled up with Jessie and Natalie.

Stewards direct the car to the front of the observatory, where the red carpet stretches the length of the gardens and then up to the huge, ornate front door.

'It's such a beautiful building,' Natalie says, and she's right, it really is. Long and white, it has three black domes, one at each end and one in the middle. The main door and all the windows are floodlit, making the whole building look like it's glowing.

We get out of the car and start to walk up the red carpet. Just seeing the cameras – or rather the photographers – makes my palms sweat. I realise I'm crushing some of my dress in my hands and smooth it out over my legs.

'Are you OK?' Jessie asks me.

I take a deep breath and nod.

Flashes go off as we go inside the building, but there's no shouting and it's not frightening like it was with Alex. It's an entirely different atmosphere.

Inside, the circular foyer is full of people, laughing and talking, clinking glasses. I still manage to spot Mum and Michael immediately. They come straight over and Michael grabs us drinks as a waiter passes with a tray.

'Where's Oscar?' I ask.

Michael looks around. 'Outside, I think. He's here somewhere. You'll find him.'

Jessie and I follow signs back outside to the terrace. The sun's almost completely gone so the sky is a gorgeous mix of purple, orange and pink. LA's lights stretch pretty much as far as the eye can see. Neither of us speaks, we just lean on the white wall and look out across the view.

'Not too high for you?' Jessie asks, smiling.

In New York, I refused to go up the Empire State Building with her because I don't like heights, but this is different. The wall is high and solid and there's no way I could fall. It's the falling I'm afraid of, not the height.

'It's gorgeous, isn't it?' I say, smiling.

She nods. 'I had no idea.'

Me neither.

The terrace is busy. I see a couple of actors I recognise from *Gossip Girl*, Jessie points out someone who was on *The Hills* and someone she thinks might be Morgan Freeman – he's really into astronomy, apparently. Oscar told me.

'Are you going to go and find him?' Jessie says, as if she's read my mind.

'I think I need another drink first,' I say.

'Oh, you do not. Stop being so pathetic. We're in this incredibly romantic place, you look gorgeous and you're mad about him. So just go and tell him. Or I will.'

*

As I walk back down the terrace, I see the Hollywood sign in the distance. I didn't know you could see it from here. It's so much smaller than I expected it to be. I turn to go back inside the building and see Oscar coming out through the enormous doors.

He's wearing a tux with a red tie and cummerbund and he looks absolutely gorgeous. He sees me and grins and I feel butterflies burst to life in my stomach.

As I walk up to him, I'm trying to think of what to say, but my head is empty. I'm just staring at his smile.

'You look amazing,' he says.

I look down at myself and then back up at him. 'So do you.'

We both grin.

'I think we need to talk,' I tell him.

He nods. 'I know just the place. Come with me.'

I follow him up the staircase at the side of the building. There are a couple of people posing for photos in front of the view, but I follow Oscar around towards the back and then it's just us.

'I've been freaking out,' I tell him. I look out at the

view, at all the lights stretching out into the distance, towards the ocean, towards where I live now.

'Because of the kiss?' he says.

I look at him and then back at the view. 'Yes, because of the kiss. I'm so sorry I pulled away like that. You just took me by surprise.'

'I know. It wasn't my best work.'

I laugh. 'The whole thing took me by surprise. Not just the kiss. You've changed, you know? You've kept all the funny, quirky, weird—'

'I think "eccentric" is the polite word.'

'Well, you've still got all the eccentric bits, but now you've got this amazing smile and sexy arms and you're so confident and together. I didn't expect it.'

'You're just as gorgeous as you always were,' he says. 'But now you're here.'

My stomach flips over almost painfully. I turn away from the view and look at Oscar.

He takes a deep breath and then he says, 'I really like you. When you left with Alex that night, I really wanted to punch him. And you know that wouldn't have ended well for me.'

'I'm so sorry about that. I think I only invited him

because I was scared to be alone with you.'

Oscar laughs. 'You could've just said no when I asked you to come to the Wok.'

'I didn't want to do anything to jeopardise our friendship.'

'I know. And I felt such an idiot when I kissed you that day. I didn't mean to do it like that. I was going to ask you out or at least say something, but then you were there and I really wanted to and I know it freaked you out. I just didn't really know how to fix it. It's hard to say "I really like you and if you don't like me the same way I'll be devastated, but I really want us to stay friends. Will you be OK with me sniffing your hair every now and then?"'

'You could've put it in a song,' I say, grinning.

'You think I didn't try?' He smiles.

We stare at each other.

'So,' I say, 'if you wanted to sniff my hair now, that would be fine with me.'

'Really?' he says. 'And what if I wanted to kiss you?'

I don't bother answering, I just kiss him. Oscar.

His hands slide round my waist and I move mine

up his back. One of his hands moves up into my hair and I press up closer to him. Then I hear someone coming up the steps and I pull away. Oscar and I lean back against the wall while a woman with spiky white hair takes photos of the view with an enormous camera, pretending we're not there. All the hairs are standing up on the back of my neck.

'I spoke to my dad,' I say.

'Really? That's great.' He hooks his index finger around mine and we just stand like that, holding fingers. It's nice.

'Yeah. I told him how pissed off I was that he left, but how I want him to be happy so I'm trying to get over it.'

'That sounds...promising.'

I laugh. 'I'm paraphrasing. I said some nice stuff too.'

Oscar hooks his middle finger with mine.

'I think that was part of why I had such a hard time with this,' I say, lifting up our hands.

'Because of your dad?'

I nod. 'I really thought I'd lost him, you know? I didn't know if I could ever forgive him. And it's been so good with you since we got here... I didn't want to risk losing you too.'

'That's not going to happen,' Oscar says.

'It might,' I say.

'OK, it might,' he says, 'but let's promise to try really, really hard for it not to.'

'OK,' I say.

'OK,' he says, smiling.

The woman finishes taking photos and goes back down the steps. I look at Oscar.

He grins back at me. 'So this is nice.'

I laugh. 'Don't make it weird.'

'Well, it is a bit weird. I mean, I've been thinking about this for years and now...'

'For years? Seriously?'

'You didn't know?'

'I had no idea.'

'Well, I was trying to be subtle. Keep it low key, you know.'

'You did a good job,' I say, smiling.

We look at each other for a few seconds and he glances down at my mouth. I look at his. It's nice. He's definitely grown into it. I kiss him again.

*

I don't know how long we're up there kissing, but by the time we stop it's completely dark and I'm utterly flustered.

'I think I need to sit down,' Oscar says, dropping one last kiss just under my ear – it sends tingles through my entire body.

'I think there are some seats near the food,' I say, but before I've even finished the sentence, Oscar's sitting down on the floor.

I sit next to him. He puts his arm around me and I snuggle against him. He smells lovely. Familiar. Like Oscar.

'Look,' he says, pointing.

It's a full moon. I hadn't even realised. And it's clear enough to see the stars.

'One day you'll be up there,' I say.

'I'll give you a wave,' he says.

'I really hope you get there,' I say. 'I bet you will.'

'I bet you will too,' Oscar says.

'Where?'

'Wherever you want to go.'

I kiss him again.

Epilogue

I meet Oscar by the duck pond. He's leaning over the railings chatting to the ducks as if they can actually understand him. Completely barmy. I wrap my arms around his waist from behind and rest my head between his shoulders.

'Come here,' he says. 'I can't kiss you if you're back there.'

I kiss the back of his neck. 'But I can kiss you.'

He grabs me and swings me round into a dip. I howl, laughing, and, I admit, shriek a bit. I don't want to be dropped on the pavement.

'Cover your eyes,' he says to the ducks. 'This may get a bit steamy.'

He pulls me to my feet and I look over at the ducks, half-expecting them to have their wings over their faces. I'm becoming as mad as Oscar.

Oscar pulls me against him and kisses me and I grab hold of the railing for support. We've done a lot of kissing over the past few months and it has all been utterly excellent. I can't believe I spent so many years not kissing Oscar. If I'd known what I was missing, I would've jumped him back home in Manchester.

We say goodbye to the ducks – I think they appreciate it – and, holding hands, walk back to the canal and then head for the beach.

Oscar and I cross the bridge and the main road and then walk down one of the narrow walk streets that leads to the beach.

'How did your class go?' Oscar asks me.

I'm enrolled in school and absolutely love it. I go to Venice High, which was used for the movie *Grease*. Bex and I were obsessed with that movie a couple of years ago, so it's pretty surreal that I go there now. They're running art classes for extra credit and the first one was yesterday.

'I loved it,' I tell him.

'I knew you would,' he says, hugging me against him.

As we turn onto the Boardwalk, a girl crosses in front of us and I realise it's Tabby. She's wearing a mini dress, carrying her shoes in one hand and talking on the phone.

'Walk of shame?' Oscar whispers to me and I grin.

I take a quick snap of her back view with my phone. My project for the art class is 'community' and I'm planning to sketch the things I see around Venice.

We walk along the Boardwalk towards Santa Monica. I take a few more photos for my project and then, when Oscar picks a spot to busk, I sit on the grass embankment behind him and take out my sketchbook.

I'm supposed to be sketching the crowd, but I find myself sketching Oscar instead. I can't believe I used to have to ask myself if I thought he was attractive. Now I find him utterly gorgeous. His face is interesting and funny and so familiar – I never get tired of looking at it.

I still can't quite believe I had to come halfway across the world to fall in love with someone I've known for most of my life, but I'm not all that surprised. I think it was in the stars. Or is that too cheesy?

THE END

Acknowledgements

Thank you to...

My agent, Alice, for having my back.

My editor, Caitlin, for pushing me to make this book SO MUCH better. Even if she did make me take out an *S Club 7* reference.

Thy Bui and Mike Lemanski for the gorgeous cover. I love it even more than the last one, which I wouldn't have thought possible.

Stella for accompanying me to LA, driving me everywhere, not complaining when her feet were reduced to bloody stumps and being an all-round-fabulous travelling companion and friend. Where shall we go next?

Anstey Spraggan for being my travel guru (and dim sum orderer).

Beki Hobbs for the *Stellar Highway* suggestion.

Sally Lawton and Anis Khan for showing me round the theatre and inspiring an important scene in *Jessie Hearts NYC*. I forgot to thank them last time and I felt AWFUL about it.

My online writing sisters: Sophia Bennett, Cat Clarke, Keren David, Susie Day, Fiona Dunbar, Tamsyn Murray, Gillian Philip, Luisa Plaja, Kay Woodward.

My *other* online writing sisters (I'm very lucky): Anstey, Claire, Clodagh, Debs, Emily, Fionnuala, Helen, Jacqui, Michele, Paula, Sarah, Trina, Zoe.

Laura (Sisterspooky) and Raimy (Readaraptor) for cheerleading, butt-kicking and for being THE BEST first readers, and Steffi for being the first pre-orderer!

All the lovely book bloggers whose dedication and enthusiasm are so inspiring.

Everyone who's bought or borrowed my previous books.

Melissa Cox for being so incredibly supportive.

Alex, Anne-Marie, Diane, Erin, Jenni, Kate, Stephanie, Susan and Tanya for making Twitter such a lovely place to spend…almost all of my time.

My in-laws, Enid and Andrew, for always being more than happy to take Joe off my hands, even under the most difficult circumstances.

The staff at Starbucks, Blackburn, for not asking me to leave when I muttered dialogue to myself, banged my head on my laptop, or sat for three hours over two lattes.

My family: Leanne, Steve, Jake, Toby, Aunty Barb, Uncle John and Aunty Phyl.

But most of all to David, Harry and Joe for never – okay, hardly ever – complaining when I hog the computer, spend all day with my nose in a book or, er, fly off to LA without them for 'research'. (Special thanks to Harry for always bigging up my books.)